# THE PRICELESS GIFT

# THE PRICELESS GIFT

Hemalatha Gnanasekar

KALPAZ

ISBN : 978-93-5128-021-7

Price: ₹ 210

First Published 2014

*Published by*

Kalpaz Publications
C-30, Satyawati Nagar,
Delhi-110052
Ph. : 9212142040
E-mail: kalpaz@hotmail.com

*Laser Typesetting* : Krishna Kumar Kanhaiya, Delhi
*Printed at* : G. Print Process, Delhi

**Cataloging in Publication Data--DK**
Courtesy: D.K. Agencies (P) Ltd. <docinfo@dkagencies.com>

**Gnanasekar, Hemalatha,** 1965-
The priceless gift / by Hemalatha Gnanasekar.
p. cm.
Novel.
ISBN 9789351280217

1. Hotels--Employees--Fiction. 2. Indic fiction (English). I. Title.

DDC 823.92 23

**DEDICATED**

**TO**

**SHIRDI SAI BABA**

# PREFACE

These days, Sexual Abuse - the heartless tyranny of the powerful against the helpless and the unfortunate - is becoming rampant in our society too. However, the victims do not wish to admit it openly. They repress all their emotions and endure it silently. As a result of this, they are unable to develop healthy relationships for fear of trusting anyone. Filled with depression, they ultimately turn out to be loners.

Yet there are quite a few who stop dwelling on their bitter past and come to terms with their life. Priya is one such character who is undergoing a low phase of her life. She is sexually exploited at her workplace and gets into the family way. Unable to bear the shock, her mother passes away in heart attack. Down in the dumps, Priya is overwhelmed with doubts, fears and sorrow and is not sure where she is heading. After crying over the loss of her mother who meant the world to her she tries to move on.

Succor comes from an unknown source to her. Priya places entire trust in her neighbour's daughter who had come to visit her mother during vacation and accompanies her to Mumbai. On her advice she gives birth to Vikram and once again with a strong inner strength takes up the job of a nude model in order to bring up her son comfortably.

Life continues to put Priya through extremely challenging moments. Her son's job brings her back to Chennai her home town. One day, Vikram brings home a middle-aged man whom he had befriended and Priya finds herself face to face with Vijay, the man who had wronged her. For the first time in his life Vikram sees his mother lose her temper. Without basic courtesy she asks him to leave and Vikram is confused about his mother's rudeness. He keeps prodding her for the reasons for her bad temper and finally Priya is forced to divulge the truth to him that he was the cause of ruining her life and unfortunately happens to be his own father. Vijay is now a heart broken man who is bereaving the loss of his family in the Tsunami.

Vikram is engulfed with various emotions. On realizing the bitter truth from his mother, at first Vikramis traumatized by the fact that he has a father whom all along he had thought dead. Eventually, he is enraptured over this and pleads with his mother to give up her anger and proceed with life by forgiving him. Though Vikram is the apple of her eye, she is unrelenting and does not wish to get involved with the man who had been unfair with her. Vijay having taken a fascination of his son, persuades her to forgive him for now he longs for a settled life with her but Priya continues to be repulsive. One day he comes to see her with a wonderful bait which exerts a pull on her and Priya is spontaneously drawn towards it. Does this priceless gift woo her into submission ?

# 1

# THE PRICELESS GIFT

The Venkateswara Quality Inn was as usual bustling with activity; with people coming in and going out continuously. Vijay, the owner of the hotel was quietly sitting, watching the happenings. All of a sudden, his eyes fell on the young lad, who was just entering the hotel and at once his entire system revved up. The boy, probably in his early Twenties was new to the area and had been coming here regularly every night for over a week. Vijay was rather perplexed as to why his heart was going out to him whenever he happened to see him. He could also not understand why he was engulfed with strong feelings of love and affection towards this boy; as if he had known him all his life. Today, he was inclined to find out, more than ever. For the first time in two years, *Vijay felt the urge to talk to someone!* Slowly, he got up from his chair and started walking towards the table where boy was sitting.

Being a mother-less child, Vijay was brought up by his father who had spoilt him with too much love and pampering So much so that he had all along got everything done his way. Even in his mid-forties, he lacked dignity and manners and had never learnt to be pious. He was puffed up with self-conceit and pride and thought that he had everything in his life that one could ask for. Vijay had never known what it was to be in need of something until the day tragedy struck him. It happened on the day when Ramya was celebrating her thirteenth birthday. Vijay had taken his daughter to The Marina beach to watch the sunrise. Swathi, his wife was keeping a watch on her, sitting on the shore. Vijay was walking around with his cell-phone, talking to one of his close friends. Ramya was enjoying the tickle of sand and water under her feet. She saw a few catamarans far away and within a few minutes, the catamarans reached the shore and the fishermen embarked from them with their huge catches. Curious to see the fishes, Ramya followed them. Immediately the men squatted on the sands and divided the fishes into various categories. Several wholesalers surrounded the fishermen and started bidding for them. In a jiffy they sold all the fishes and left the place after fastening the catamarans together on the shore. Ramya quickly jumped into the catamarans and began playing inside. She called out to her mother to join her and as she walked towards her daughter, Swathi pointed out the rising sun to Ramya. "Wow! Look at that daddy. It looks as if the sun is coming out from the sea!" Ramya shrieked is excitement on seeing her father coming towards them. Vijay joined in her excitement and after a few minutes told her that it was time to return home. But Ramya pleaded him that she wished to play in the water for some more time and he relented.

Ramya ran and dipped her feet in the cool water once again and was joined by both her parents shortly. Swathi noticed that the waves were getting violent suddenly and she warned the father and daughter not to go deep into the sea. Just as she was saying this, she saw huge waves rising high in the middle of the sea forming giant walls. Slowly, it was coming closer and closer to them. All around, people started running helter-skelter screaming in fright. Filled with panic, Vijay lifted Ramya and ran towards the catamarans, holding Swathi's hand. He held the catamaran in a strong grip while his wife and daughter held onto him for support. As they stood huddled together, with their hearts in their mouth, the violent waves were already close behind them. The catamarans started getting ripped apart by the strong water currents. Even before comprehending what was happening, Vijay saw his wife and daughter being washed, away from him and abruptly drawn into the deep sea. He ran behind them for a short distance, screaming aloud and was very soon dragged into the ferocious sea in a similar manner. But as luck would have it, Vijay was swept back to the shore by another violent wave and he lay there unconscious for a long time. When at last he regained consciousness, he made an attempt to slowly get up. Confused over the clamor and din around him, he stood there paralysed in shock at what he saw. There were dead bodies everywhere and people were wailing aloud for their dear ones. Vijay immediately made a frantic search for his wife and daughter. There was no sign of either of them. Having lost all hope, he sat down on the sand letting out an ear-shattering scream.

"Oh! God!!! How can you be so cruel and heartless? Why did you take away my loving daughter and wife, leaving me all alone? Why did you spare me? I should have gone along with them too! Why am I still alive?"

The tragedy had sent Vijay's life into doldrums. He was constantly in a state of distress for he had no one, whom he could call his own now. His mother had died when he was just five years old. His father passed away soon after his marriage. And now his whole family was gone Very often the question as to why God had saved him kept coming to his mind. The incident however transformed Vijay. From a very dominating person he became a much subdued one. His workmen who dreaded even to face him were now feeling sorry for his loss and were filled with empathy towards him.

Though the wheel of time had taken a quick turn and it was almost two years now, Vijay continued to be in a melancholic mood always. He still woke up with cold sweats and nightmares. He kept hearing the waves crushing around him and the heart rending cries of his wife and daughter as they were forcibly swept away from him. Withdrawing himself into a shell, he often remained aloof and hardly spoke to anyone. But now, he was surprised that his heart was melting at the sight of this boy and so he was determined to find out the cause today.

# 2

"Are you new to this place?" Vijay asked the boy as he approached his table."Yes" the boy nodded.

"Where do you hail from?" Vijay pursued.

"Mumbai"

"You are a *Mumbaite* and you understand Tamil?"

"We belong to Chennai only. We had to move to Mumbai to eke out our leaving. Now that I have got a job here, we came back home." The boy replied.

"I see! What's your name you said?" Vijay asked rather absent-mindedly.

"I never told you my name yet", he said flashing a grin as he stood up. And before leaving, he added, "My name is Vikram".

The next day also, as soon as Vikram turned up, Vijay smiled at him. He was anxious to continue chatting with him. He got up swiftly and while following him, he said, "You seem to have come late today." "You are right indeed." Vikram said as he sat down.

"I had been sleeping and my mother did not bother to wake me up. When I shouted at her, she coolly told me that she did not wish to disturb me." Vikram further explained.

"Sleeping? At this time of the day?" Vijay was getting curious. "Of course, my biological clock is tuned like that now. I work in an IT company and I have to work and slog the whole night and sleep during the day."

"Don't you like your mother's cooking? I see you here almost every day." Enquired Vijay "Actually, she cooks hot meals in the morning and in the night, she takes the left overs and has to prepare tiffin just for me. I tell her not to strain herself and hence come here for dinner every night. After all, my mother had undergone a lot of hardships in order to educate me and now it is my turn to keep her happy."

"A responsible son indeed!" Vijay patted him on his back as he turned to leave.

They bonded very easily and were in sync with each other. Vikram did not mind his curiosity and patiently answered all his questions. Whenever Vikram walked into the hotel, Vijay made it a point to exchange a few words with him. Their friendship blossomed day after day so much so that Vijay looked forward to this time of the day when he could have a small talk with Vikram.

# 3

One evening, it was getting very cloudy and it began to rain heavily all of a sudden. Vijay was standing at the entrance of his hotel, basking in the unusual summer rain after a rather hot day. The downpour very soon created puddles of water on the roads. As he stood there blankly staring into the dark night, he saw Vikram maneuvering his way through the puddles. Despite carrying an umbrella, he was fully wet and Vijay directed him to sit under the fan so that his clothes would dry quickly. Further, he took out his handkerchief from his pocket and offered it to him. Vikram thanked him for his kindness and started rubbing his hands with it first. Then as he was wiping his face, Vijay was surprised to see a golden watch glittering on his wrist.

"Is that a new watch you are wearing?" He asked him continuing to admire the watch.

"Not really! In fact, this watch is as old as me. Actually, my mother doesn't like to give this to anyone. She would often tell me that it is a priceless gift that my father had given to her before his death. Hence, she treasures it in her cupboard; never letting me lay my hands on it. Today, being my birthday, she asked me to wear it to the temple."

"Can I have a look at it?" Vijay extended his hand.

"Oh sure!" Vikram said as he unfastened his watch and handed it to him.

Vijay examined the golden watch closely; turning it from side to side. When he saw the name *G. Venketeswaran* embossed on the rear side of the watch, he became stupefled. It was his father's name; after whom this hotel was named as *The Venketeswara Quality Inn.* What baffied him was the fact as to how it had landed on this boy's hand. He stood there rooted to the ground, lost in thoughts. Slowly things unfolded before him. He remembered the day when his father had painfully given away his costly golden watch to Parvathy, who had worked with them as a cook for over flfteen years. It was his ancestral property which was so dear to him and which he had all along considered a symbol of luck. Vijay was dumbfounded. He stared at Vikram in utter disbelief. The memories of Priya who had worked under him for just a month, came fiooding to his mind. Suddenly, Vijay was unable to think coherently. Returning the watch to Vikram, he said, "It's a nice watch. Keep it safely." He then abruptly turned to leave, without his usual chat with him.

# 4

Back home that night, Vijay could not sleep. How unique, are the ways of God, he thought. Was this the reason that he was overwhelmed with feelings on having met the boy before and hence had taken an instant liking for him. What could one call this? Fate? Providence? His mind was in total chaos. He paced the room from one end to the other restlessly. He deliberated at length on the atrocities he had committed in his life. *He had just taken over the management of "The Venketeswara Quality Inn" from his father. Vijay was a contrast to his father who was an epitome of kindness. He behaved in an arrogant manner and everyone became so terrified of him. He did everything according to his own whims and fancies unconcerned about the hateful feelings he was evoking among his workmen.*

It was during this time that Priya, who was enjoying her vacation after completing her Twelfth standard examinations joined The Venketeswara Quality Inn on her mother's advice. She was to assist Vijay in carrying out small errands that he assigned to her. The moment Vijay's eyes fell on her he was head over heels in love with her. But how could he tell his father that he was madly in love with this girl. Surely, his father would never approve of his marrying a worker in his hotel and would start lecturing him about social inequality and castes of which he was very particular. Hence, he started to misuse his powers by constantly harassing the girl both physically and mentally and ultimately ruining her life.

God is indeed watching everything, he realised. It has indeed been rightly said that "God sees but waits". How true it has turned out to be in his case. He had punished him cruelly by snatching away his family from him, leaving him in despair. For the last two years, ever since the tragedy struck, Vijay had been tormented with the question as to why God had spared him all alone. Today, he got his answer to that. To seek redemption from all the sins he had done in the past. For this, he had to first of all meet Priya and seek forgiveness from her.

# 5

The next day, when Vikram came to the hotel, Vijay gave him some time to settle down. Then he went to him and said, "I am really upset with you. Yesterday was your birthday and you did not offer any cake or even a chocolate to me."

"I am sorry about that." Vikram responded quickly. Then he added, "But you could have asked me." Vikram was making things easier for him. "Oh, should I ask you for everything. Well then, can I come home tonight for a cup of tea?" he drawled. "Oh, sure, why not?" Vikram said, but immediately retracted, "Actually, I am on my way to work now. Tomorrow is Saturday and is a holiday for me. I shall take you home tomorrow evening."

Vijay was happy that Vikram had at least consented to take him home. He was now getting very anxious. He wondered, what Priya's reaction would be on seeing him. Surely, she would lose her composure and fly into a rage. But Vijay was geared up, to bear the brunt of her anger. For, right now he had lost all energy to fight back. In a good-natured manner he wished to justify her that his indulgences were all due to his youthful stupidity. Yet, he had his own reservations. Would Priya be willing to forgive him? Because, unless she pardons him, he would not be absolved for his sins.

# 6

As Priya cut open the milk packet and started boiling the milk, she smiled to herself. Chennai had indeed transformed her son, she thought happily.

While they used to live in Mumbai, Vikram hardly spoke to anyone. Priya was very concerned about her son's introvert behaviour and worried whether he would turn out to be a hermit. But after coming to Chennai, she found that Vikram was slowly coming out of his shell. During week-ends, he entertained her with jokes and anecdotes that took place at his workplace. And today, he was bringing home a friend! She was glad about this tremendous change in her son.

Priya was just about to pour the tea into the flask when Vikram came in and announced excitedly about the arrival of his friend and requested her to bring some tea and snacks. Priya carried the serving tray containing hot *pakodas* and tea to the living room.

When her eyes fell on the man sitting in front of her she was stumped. Her smile vanished quickly and her face turned pale. She glanced at him once more to ascertain herself.

*Yes, It is very much him; he who had ruined her life.* Although, twenty long years had passed by, his features had not changed and hence she was able to recognise him instantly. *You don't forget the face of the person who has harmed you for a lifetime!* Suddenly, her stomach began to churn and her throat constricted. She remembered all the atrocities he had done to her in the past. She stood there paralysed in shock. *Why was he here? What did he intend to do now? As if the damage he had done to her and the sufferings she had undergone on account of him was not enough?*

The moment Vikram informed her that he was offered a job in Chennai, her mind was in great turmoil. She hated Chennai. She had once fled from Chennai, leaving behind everything. To her it was a place of hardship and mental agony.

Priya was eight years old, when her father died in an accident. Her mother was forced to step into his shoes and became the bread winner of the family. She had to go out for a job leaving Priya all alone at home. While her mother was working very hard to eke out their living, Priya would be sitting at home, deprived of any love.

Her mother had brought her up strictly giving her no opportunity to voice her opinion or complain about anything. This being her background, when Vikram was born, Priya decided to be very kind and a loving mother to her son. She was very lenient and let him have his way on all matters. But when Vikram told her that he had got a job in Chennai and that they were going back to their home town, she became sad for she never wished to leave Mumbai. Somehow, to her Mumbai was safer where no one cared about what you are doing nor pried into your life. Everyone were too busy with their own lives. She had been able to bring up her son without much difficulty. Reserving her doubts and fears to herself, she obliged to her son's wishes and accompanied him to Chennai.

Now, seeing this man here in front of her, she thought that her hunch had indeed been right. Her fear that she might run into this man who had destroyed her life turned out to be true. Her heart was thumping; making her breathless. Looking at her son with wide and troubled eyes, she asked, “Is this man only your friend? Did you not get any other person in whole world who is of your age to be friends with?” She questioned almost screaming.

His mother’s reaction was a kick in the teeth for Vikram. He became upset over her rude behaviour. However, ignoring her question, he silently took the tray from her trembling hands and offered the snacks to Vijay and sat down beside him; praying that she should return to the kitchen immediately without creating any more of a scene.

While a storm was brewing in Priya’s mind, Vijay coolly started relishing the *pakodas*, as if nothing had happened around. After all, he had come fully prepared to face any flare-ups that may ensue during his meeting.

Not getting any response from her son, Priya raised her voice again.

“Vikram, did you not hear me? Is this ruthless fellow your friend? Tell me how did you fall into his trap?”

Vikram had never seen his mother behave in such an arrogant manner. His mother’s outburst was incoherent to him and he wondered why she was speaking like thisy all of a sudden. In a very innocent manner, he asked, “Is there any age bar for friendship? Why are you so offended about this?” Her son’s rejoinder infuriated her. “Vikram”, she threatened. “I hate this man to the core and do not wish to see his face. Will you please ask him to go out?”

Vikram became so embarrassed by his mother’s rage. He was lost and could not understand why she was yelling and for a moment wished to turn into a drop of water and seep inside the earth. Realising Vikram’s predicament, Vijay stood up at once after placing the tea cup on the table, he said; “Don’t argue with your mother. I shall take leave now”. He then started walking towards the door but stopped abruptly. Standing at the door step, he looked at Priya with pleading eyes and said, “I have not come here to cause any trouble. I am desperately sorry for whatever I have done. God had indeed punished me enough for all the wrong I had done to you by snatching away my family. I was in a state of mourning when I chanced to meet

Vikram, who was a great solace to me. It was only after I saw the gold watch my father had given to your mother that I realised you were back in Chennai and came to see you and seek forgiveness from you; for only then can I find salvation in this life."

Unable to comprehend what was transpiring in his house between the two of them, Vikram stood there giving a confused what is happening here look at his mother. At the mention of the golden watch, Priya was flabbergasted. Her insides clenched and rolled all at once. Shutting her ears, she screamed on top of her voice, "I am in no mood to listen to you now". Please leave my house immediately or else...Patting Vikram on his shoulder, Vijay said, "Well, I shall make a move right away before your mother flings something at me."

# 7

Though Priya was very lenient with her son, she would often counsel him about good manners and behaviour. One thing she was very particular about was that her son should not fall into bad company. She would keep harping on the same thing to him, "While choosing your friends be very careful. Bad friends would teach you all kinds of vices like smoking, drinking etc. and ultimately ruin your life. There is nothing wrong in having no friends at all rather than having even one bad friend who might spoil your life." Hearing this time and again, the advice got ingrained in him and Vikram tried to keep to himself most of the time.

But Vijay had volunteered to come and have a chat with him and Vikram could do nothing to stop him. Moreover, he was in a grievous mood and was sharing his tales of sorrow and Vikram only empathised with him. Very soon, Vijay became an endearing person for him and despite their age difference; their friendship grew by leaps and bounds. His mother's misdemeanor irked Vikram and he wished to take it out on her. After seeing Vijay off, he entered the house seething in anger.

"Ma, have you gone insane all of sudden? Is age such a crucial factor for friendship? Do you want to know how my peers behave? All of them smoke, drink and always talk about girls, sex and pubs. To them, life is all about having fun that too at the cost of others' misery. I bet you won't like any one of them either. This gentleman I brought home has somehow found a place in my heart. He has lost his family and is in a gloomy mood. Instead of being compassionate towards him, you dismissed him in an impolite manner. Is it fair on your part to do so?"

Priya was already boiling inside. Now her son's criticism was only adding fuel to fire. "Vikram" she yelled. "I don't owe any explanation to you, understand! Don't go to that hotel again and do not talk to that wretched guy. And this is an order!"

Irked by his mother's obstinacy, Vikram asked, "Why are you making such a great fuss over such a trivial matter?"

Provoked by his rejoinder, she said, "Vikram, don't argue with me. All I want is your implicit obedience in this matter."

Infuriated, Vikram shouted, "Well, in that case tell me why I should not meet him. Do you know him already? What is the reason for you to detest him ?"

"How dare you talk to me like this?" Priya was becoming hysterical over her son's non-compliance. Very soon, her anger exploded into violence and she lifted the empty tea cup from the fioor and fiung it across to him. The cup hit Vikram's forehead gashing his skin. As blood started oozing out from the wound, Vikram stood there wincing in pain.

Realizing her folly and suddenly feeling ashamed for her impulsive behaviour, Priya ran to wipe the blood with her sari. But Vikram shoved her away and screamed on the top of his voice, "Stop treating me like a kid anymore!" Further, pointing a finger at her he continued, "Unless you answer my questions, I am not going to heed to you. You cannot prevent me from seeing him. No one can. Not even God!" With these words, he stormed out of the house, banging the door behind him.

# 8

For the first time in her life, Priya realised that Vikram had outgrown her. She had all along been hiding facts from him and Vikram was now twisting her arms. It was up to her to set right the misunderstanding that had cropped up between them by justifying her outburst. For this, she has to divulge the whole past story to him. The time has at last come for her to tell the truth to her son. This being an arduous task, she wondered how she was going to do it. Where would she begin? As she lay on her bed deliberating on how best she could make her point, the memory of her past life loomed large in front of her like the fiash back in a movie Priya was Eighteen years old then, and she had given her twelfth standard board exams and was awaiting her results. Her one and only aim in life was to finish her graduation and go out for a job. Right from childhood, she had seen her mother slog from the crack of dawn to dusk and Priya wished to relieve her from hardship by being able to support her financially. It was during this time that Parvathy came home one day with some good news for her daughter.As soon as she stepped into the house, she asked her daughter, "Are you interested in taking up a job during the vacation, instead of just whiling away your time? You would be given a salary of Rs. 2000 per month" "Oh, sure, I would be glad to go for a job!" Priya at once jumped at the prospect. "In that case, come along with me tomorrow morning to *The Venketeswara Quality Inn.*" Her mother said and went to prepare dinner; pleased that her daughter had consented to spend her holidays in a useful manner.

# 9

Parvathy had been working as a cook in *The Venketeswara Quality Inn* for the past fifteen years ever since her husband passed away. Mr. Venketeswaran, the owner of this hotel was a man with a heart of gold. Doing good and helping others gave him a sense of self-worth. He was very kind to his workers and took good care of them. He paid them good salary which he enhanced year after year. During festivals and occasions, he spent money lavishly by giving them a huge bonus. Anyone who worked extra hours was paid an overtime. Also, from time to time, he met each of his staff individually and redressed their grievances if any. Everyone felt very comfortable working here and no one ever thought of leaving their jobs. In fact, they exerted themselves out of their own interest as though the hotel belonged to them.

This was one of the reasons why Parvathy, despite her experience and excellent culinary skills, refused to accept better offers that came her way and continued working here. Somehow, she felt safe and secure in this place and hence never felt the need to move. There had been no dearth of food and clothing and she had easily been able to educate her daughter till twelfth standard and was now planning to send her to a good college. However, her neighbours often criticized her. They asked her why she was working so hard toiling so much without even spending enough time with her only daughter. Parvathy managed to silence them by retorting, "It is only for my loving daughter that I am straining so hard. I am able to give her three square meals a day and also send her to a convent school. I have got no Godfather to help me but my own hands. Without such hard work, all this would not have been possible. Once she settles in a good job, I would retire from my service and take care of my daughter and her kids. But right now, I have no time for any luxuries."

Though Venketeswaran portrayed himself to be a cheerful person, but inside he was devastated at heart. When his wife passed away at a very young age, leaving her five year old son under his care, he became heart broken. His close friends advised him to marry again but Venketeswaran was not for it. He did not want his son to get a step-motherly treatment and hence remained single all his life.

He appointed a live-in servant, exclusively for taking care of his son. The old lady was very kind and she took good care of Vijay. Very soon, Vijay stopped asking for his mother. Being a mother-less child, Venketeswaran pampered him a lot. He let him have his way in all matters and ultimately spoilt him. Thus, Vijay turned out to be an unruly child.

At school, during every parent and -teachers meeting, the class teachers complained to Venketeswaran that his son was very mischievous and that he bullied his classmates frequently. Venketeswaran would cut a sorry figure always and assure the teachers that he would discipline his son. Later at home when he admonished his son, Vijay would quickly retort that he would behave well hereafter. However, he never kept his word and within a few days, he would return to being the same. Thus, things came back to square one.

Vijay continued to be incorrigible even in college. He ragged the new comers from time to time and was once suspended from college for this. Venketeswaran had a tough time convincing the principal and getting his son readmitted. This time, he was so upset with Vijay that he had stopped talking to him. It was only after three days that Vijay decided to take the first step in compromising with his father. He met him in the hotel and apologised for his bad behaviour and promised him that he would not repeat this henceforth. This time he kept his promise.

After finishing college, though Vijay went out for a job, he could not stick on to one particular place for long. Within a short time, he quarreled with his boss and tendered his resignation. Vijay was becoming a pain in the neck for his father and Venketeswaran was worried about his future. His son was already Twenty five years old and had not yet settled in life. Without a permanent job, Venketeswaran was also not able to find a suitable alliance for his son. While pondering over this one day, an idea struck him.

He decided to handover the hotel to his son and retire from his duties. By placing a huge responsibility on his shoulders, Venketeswaran believed that his son would turn over a new leaf. He wished to pay attention to his health which he had so far neglected. Besides, he was planning to involve himself in religious and social activities.

When his staff heard about their boss stepping down, they were alarmed. However, Venkeswaran allayed their fears by telling them that he was not handing over the hotel to any outside party but to his own son. Further, he assured them that he would be available anytime and they were free to approach him with their personal problems.

# 10

When Venketeswaran informed Vijay about his intention of handing over the hotel to him, he was very ecstatic. Appreciating his father's magnanimity and kind-heartedness he vouched to him that he would do his best and endeavor to take *The Venketeswara Quality Inn* to greater heights. Vijay could not believe that his father was entrusting him with such an enormous responsibility and this time he was hell-bent upon living up to his father's expectations.

He took up the management of the hotel in good earnest. His MBA qualification was an added advantage to him. For the first few weeks, he was involved with the work of revamping and modernisation of the rather run down condition of the hotel. Once he had successfully refurbished the hotel, he steadily started making changes in the functioning style of the hotel.

Vijay reported to his father about the daily activities of the hotel. From time to time, he clarified his doubts and sought his advice and suggestions on areas where he wished to improvise. Seeing that his son was working with keen enthusiasm and dedication, Venketeswaran slowly stopped interfering in the day to day affairs of the hotel and let his son take independent decisions. Vijay put his heart and soul into the job and within a short span of time; he won the confidence of his father. Venketeswaran was jubilating over his son's competence and prided himself on having taken the right decision.

During his early morning walk one day, Venketeswaran chanced to meet his old friend Ramanathan. Both had been best friends and had studied together till college. While Venketeswaran had continued to live in Chennai, Ramanathan's job took him far away from his home town. Now after his retirement, he was back in Chennai. He had already conducted the marriage of his first two daughters successfully and was now in the lookout for a suitable alliance for his third daughter Swathi who had just completed her graduation. On learning that Vijay the only son of his friend was in charge of the hotel, Ramanathan slowly brought up the topic of his daughter's alliance. He asked him if he was willing to give his son in marriage to his daughter. Venketeswaran readily agreed to his proposal however added that he will have to talk to his son before giving his final approval. Happy that, at last things were falling in line, Venketeswaran was now waiting for an opportune moment to discuss the subject of marriage with his son.

Venketeswaran was an embodiment of kindness and had been very lenient with his staff. His workers enjoyed two hours of rest time between 2.00 p.m and 4.00 p.m every day. But they absconded from work according to their own whims and fancies without seeking permission. A few others came late almost every day while some of them did not even turn up for work without giving any prior information. But Venketeswaran had not once questioned his staff regarding the lapse on their part. For he had noticed that there was extreme unity and cooperation among his staff and if any one of them did not turn up for work, someone else volunteered to do their job and the functions of the hotel went about smoothly.

It had been a year since his taking over and Vijay was now well versed with his job. His father had completely severed his ties with the affairs of the hotel and Vijay started taking his own decisions on all matters concerning the running of the hotel. Unlike his father, Vijay was not prepared to tolerate the lackadaisical attitude of his workers. He brought about drastic changes without even bothering to consult his staff. First, he curtailed their rest time by one hour and gave a strict warning that no one was supposed to take leave without prior permission and non-compliance to this would result in their salaries being deducted. Also coming late to work or leaving early was strictly prohibited unless it was an emergency. He stood at the entrance every morning and reprimanded anyone who came late for work; not minding the fact that some of them were much older than him and had been working there for a long time. During the day, he went about supervising the jobs of each and every person and those who had less work to do were loaded with additional work.

The workers felt that Vijay was being very unfair with them. Further they did not like his overbearing attitude. They had all along got used to kindness and humble requests of his father. Many of the older folks left their jobs without as much as a word to Vijay. This however did not deter him in anyway. He did not mind the loss of experienced hands and unemotionally appointed youngsters in their place as replacements.

# 11

Parvathy, was neither flustered by Vijay's domineering nature nor by the reformations he was making, for she had nothing to fear. She had always been a hard worker and a staunch follower of the adage "work is worship". She also had a great reverence for Venketeswaran Vijay's father for having given her a job at the time when her life was in doldrums. Hence she valued this job very dearly. She had been working with great vigor ever since the day she joined and had immensely contributed towards the growth of *The Venketeswaran Quality Inn.*

While the other workers were engaged in gossip or having a short siesta during their rest time, Parvathy would keep by herself and be busy in the kitchen. She would either be tidying up the place or getting things ready for dinner. Many a times, Venketeswaran had chided her for laboring so hard, but Parvathy would tell him that immersing herself in work gave her solace.

Apart from her job as a cook, Parvathy extended her services to Venketeswaran by carrying out small errands for him. She had a spare key to his private room where no one else dared to enter. On reaching the hotel, she would first clean up his room. Then she would place the newspapers on his table and fill in his flasks with hot water. Immediately, on his arrival, she would bring him some coffee and breakfast.

After his retirement, Parvathy continued to do this job for Vijay. Having seen her from his childhood and also hearing from his father about her devotion and commitment to her job, Vijay never once raised his voice in front of her and was always polite to her.

One morning, Vijay was sprawling on the sofa, with newspapers scattered all around him, when Parvathy came in with a tray containing his breakfast and coffee. Vijay immediately stood up and said, "Madam, I do not want you to be doing these chores for me henceforth. You are already having enough work in the kitchen. Do you know any boy who could work as a peon for me? I am ready to pay him Rs. 2000 per month."

As she placed the tray on his table, she said, "I shall enquire with my friends in the Neighbourhood and let you know tomorrow."

The next day, early morning, Parvathy was busy cutting vegetables, when Vijay walked into the kitchen. Pouring himself some coffee from the flask which Parvathy intended to take for him shortly, he asked, "Where you successful in finding someone for me?" Taken aback by his sudden appearance Parvathy said, "Well...., I did ask a few people last night. No one is willing to come for such a meager salary." Vijay stood there silently drinking his coffee when Parvathy continued, "If it is OK with you, I shall bring my daughter to work temporarily until you find a suitable person. She has just completed her Twelfth standard Examinations and is waiting for her results. It will be another six months before I put her in some college. Right now, she is whiling away her time in front of the television the whole day."

Handing over the empty cup back to her, he said, "Ask her to come and see me tomorrow."

# 12

Priya could not sleep the whole night. She kept tossing and turning in her bed because she was too excited that she was going for a job. When her mother told her that she would even be paid a salary of Two thousand rupees a month, Priya jumped in joy and did not even bother to ask her mother the nature of job she was supposed to do. She was willing to do any kind of job and reduce her mother's financial burden. *Perhaps she could save some money for her college admission.* The next morning, she woke up along with her mother; early before sunrise and got ready to accompany her to work.

It was 9.30 in the morning, when Vijay entered his room, talking on his cell phone. Parvathy waited outside his room for him to finish his conversation. Once he was finished, she walked in with her daughter. "I have brought my daughter with me today," she said beaming with a smile.

"What's your name?" he asked turning to her.

"Priya" She said, so feebly that Vijay was hardly able to hear her.

"Didn't you have your breakfast this morning?" He sneered.

Taking cue from his remark Priya immediately repeated her name, this time a little louder.

"Well... Priya, won't you be missing your TV programmes if you come here for work? Your mother told me that you are glued to the television the whole day" He said.

"No, no, I won't be missing it. Since I have nothing to study these days, I am watching TV. Otherwise, I generally don't see much of TV." She answered.

Looking at Parvathy, he continued, "Actually, my driver has promised me to bring a boy from his village within a couple of months. Let her work here until such a time." He then stood up immediately to go on with his usual rounds to check if things were in order. Parvathy explained to her daughter about the work she was expected to do. Within a few days, Priya was able to handle the job on her own without her mother's intervention.

A week passed by and things went on smoothly for Priya. Vijay had been kind towards her and never raised his voice even once. It was only after a week that Priya came to know about his true colours.

One morning, Vijay stepped into his room and saw the fan running in full speed and the important papers he had kept on his table were scattered on the fioor. He became angry and looked around for Priya but there was no sign of her. He went to the kitchen to find out from her mother if she had turned up for work or not. When he saw Priya standing there beside her mother cutting vegetables, he yelled standing at the doorway, "What the hell are you doing here?"

Putting down the knife abruptly, Priya said, "I am just helping my mother. She is having fever and has come to work despite it."

"Are you here to work for your mother or me?" He shouted; indifferent towards her feelings. Priya stared at him in disbelief, without giving him any reply. Seeing that Vijay was in one of his bad moods, Parvathy gestured her daughter to leave the place at once. As she walked towards him, he further continued his tirade, "People in the kitchen will take good care of your mother. You are here to help me and not your mother; understood?" Silently she trailed behind him, upset over his uncaring attitude.

On the way, her body was trembling in fear when she saw him lose his temper again. This time he took a young boy to task for gossiping early in the morning without clearing a cluttered table. In a heartless manner, he slapped him so hard that made everyone turn back and look. Ordering him to tidy up the mess, he quietly walked into his room. The poor boy attended to his job crying and Priya was rather shocked that none of the workers came around to console him. All of a sudden Priya was gripped with fear at this rude behaviour.

He pulled out a chair and placed it outside his room and said, "This is your place from now. You are not supposed to move from here without my permission. Is that clear?" Priya nodded and went ahead to pick up the papers that were strewn on the fioor and stacked them on his table. She sat in her place and remained sullen for the rest of the day. She realised that she could not work under such an arrogant person for long. However, she reassured herself that it was after all her vacation job and very soon she would be leaving for college. She could stop coming here whenever she chose to do so.

# 13

A fortnight had passed very quickly and Priya was excited that after another two weeks, she would be receiving her first salary. She was sitting and dreaming about the day when she could walk home with her first salary, when all of a sudden Vijay summoned her in a loud voice. He had just finished reading the newspaper and got up for his rounds when suddenly his eyes fell on a patch of dust and a few bits of papers under his table.

When Priya came in, he asked, "Did you not sweep my room today?"

"I have swept it already." She said nonchalantly. Tweaking her nose, he pointed to the area beneath his table and asked, "Is this the way you do your work?" Priya had inadvertently skipped that portion and instantly realised that she was at fault. She stood there struggling as he was still clutching her nose with a strong grip. Tears glistened her eyes and finally seeing her gasping for breath, he took his hand off and ordered, "Go and clean up the place at once." Wiping away her tears, Priya swept the room once again.

That evening, when Priya was walking home with her mother, she was not sure if she should complain about the ill-treatment she had faced at the hands of Vijay. Because Priya was well aware of the fact that her mother never liked to listen to her grouches.

*Priya was ten years old. Her mother had packed fried rice for her in lunch, which she was never tired of eating. When Priya opened her tiffin box at school, she was shocked to find it empty. Somebody had stolen her food. She returned home famished. When her mother came back from work, she pouted, "Someone had eaten my food today and I am so hungry now." She expected that her mother would feel sorry for her but instead only received a slap. "This shows how careless you are" She scolded her. Further she berated her, "I strain myself and prepare your favourite dish and you let some bully eat it. The world is full of swindlers, waiting for an opportunity to pull your leg. It is up to you to save your skin. No one will come and help you." That was when Priya learnt her lesson in life. She bottled up all her emotions and tried to tackle her problems on her own without complaining to her mother. She understood that her mother just did not have the time to listen to her grouches.*

Of late, her mother was not keeping well. She was getting frequent bouts of fever and was feeling out of sorts. Priya did not wish to be the cause of any further worry to her. She decided not to disclose anything to her mother.

However, a few days later, when Vijay took her to task once again, Priya could not put up with it. One morning, after Vijay had just left the room for his rounds, Priya entered inside. She removed the empty cup and saucer from his table and placed it on the tray. As she swiftly turned around to take it to the kitchen, the cup and saucer slipped out of the tray and smashed on the fioor. On hearing the loud clattering noise, Vijay returned to his room.

Priya was picking up the broken pieces with trembling hands. When she saw Vijay approaching her, she became scared out of her wits.

"What is this?" He asked twisting her ear sharply.

"The cup and saucer fell off the tray" She mumbled nervously.

"I can see that for myself. Tell me how can you be so careless in doing your job?" He scolded her, pulling her closer to him.

Priya started squealing in pain and her eyes were filled with tears.

*How cruel of him to humiliate her in this manner. She had come here to assist him temporarily, obliging her mother and was being treated like a crap.*

Forcefully, she wrenched his hand away from her and screamed, "I did not do it deliberately. It just fell off from the tray by mistake."

Vijay was rather stunned by her curt rejoinder. In fact, no one spoke to him so rudely. Whenever he railed at his staff, they remained silent regardless of the fact that they were innocent. He was at once incensed by her curt reply. He slapped her hard across her face and said, "How dare you speak to me like that? I am not here to tolerate your mistakes, understand?" He then walked out heartlessly.

Priya felt a burning sensation and clutching her cheek, she stood there crying helplessly. After sometime, she washed her face and walked briskly towards the kitchen to apprise her mother about the happenings. But mid-way, she changed her mind and came back. She did not wish to harm the reputation of her mother by letting her down in her workplace, so she decided that it could wait until they reached home. For the rest of the day, she worked silently with a sullen face.

At home after dinner, she sat down beside her mother and said, "Ma, I went to work there just because you recommended me. But Vijay is behaving roughly with me like he does with the other workers. I would like to quit my job." She said regretfully.

Without a moment of hesitation, her mother said, "It is up to you. There is no any hard and fast rule that you must go for a job now. You can leave your job anytime you wish."

"I would like to discontinue from next month and shall be going only for another two days." Priya declared to her mother.

Parvathy did not ask her for any explanation. She just gave a silent nod and went to bed early as she was feeling too sick.

Priya's face brightened. She never expected that her mother would take the matter so easily. 'Another two days and then she would be a free bird!' She thought to herself.

However, her happiness was only short lived. Her mother was once again suffering with a high temperature and was groaning in acute body pain. Disheartened by this, she chided her, "Ma, please get up and come along with me to the hospital. Your self-medication has done you no good. It has only worsened your health further."

Parvathy was finding it too difficult even to stand for a long time in the kitchen and she realised that something was drastically wrong with her body. This time, she relented to her daughter and accompanied Priya to the hospital immediately.

After examining her, the doctor prescribed a few tablets to arrest the fever and wrote out a list of tests to be carried out. Just as Priya paced in the direction towards the laboratory, her mother stopped her. "We can simply buy these tablets and go home. There is no necessity for doing the blood tests right now."

It was 11.00 pm when they returned home. The next morning Priya got up very late. Her spirits dampened when she saw her mother still asleep beside her. Slowly, she started prodding her. Her mother woke up startled and sighed rather gloomily, "Oh my God! I have never before overslept like this. Perhaps it is because of the strong dosage of tablets." Further she added drowsily, "I have decided to take some rest and will not be coming today. You are already late for work, so hurry up."

Priya got ready in a haste and while grabbing a few slices of bread she told her mother, "If you are not feeling better by evening, you must get a blood test done as advised by the doctor." Her mother agreed to this. After seeing off her daughter, she went and lay down on the bed once again; upset why her health was failing her.

# 14

As Priya scurried across the road, she thought, *Another two more days and then all this hustle and bustle would come to an end!* Huffing and puffing, she reached the hotel and noticed that Vijay had already arrived. When she stepped into his room, she saw him sitting in the sofa reading the newspaper.

Immediately on his arrival, when Vijay observed that Priya was not around, he presumed that she would probably be coming along with her mother to complain about his harsh behaviour yesterday. Or worse still she must have given up her job. And when he saw her coming alone, he was rather surprised.

"Why are you late?" He asked without lifting his head. Priya evaded his question; too intimidated to speak to him. When she saw that he was seriously engrossed in his reading the paper, she sneaked out of the room silently and returned with a broom. Not having received any reply from her, Vijay looked up. Priya was sweeping the floor, bending so low that his eyes fell on her fully exposed breasts. Unable to resist his temptation, he continued to admire them for a while. Suddenly, all his emotions got stirred up and he was filled with a feverish urge to reach out and caress them. Feeling ashamed at such low thoughts of his swaying in his mind, he hastened out of the room.

It was three o'clock in the evening when Priya started getting restless. Vijay had gone out in the morning and had not yet returned. Her mother too was not around. She wished to engage herself in some work to keep her mind off from the dreary thoughts about her mother's deteriorating health condition. She decided to rearrange the furniture and dust Vijay's table which was covered with a thin layer of dust. Careful not to topple anything, she was gently wiping the table with a soft cloth when her eyes instantly fell on a glittering watch. It was a golden watch, studded with diamonds all around. The sparkling stones dazzled her eyes and Priya picked up the watch and started admiring it. *How would this grand watch look on her wrist?* An incredible urge to wear it overtook her. Giving in to her temptation, she wore it immediately and turned her hand from side to side and at all angles marveling at its splendor. *Oh! How gorgeous it looked on her wrist! One day, she would buy a similar watch, no matter what the cost!*

As she was unfastening the watch, a snorting sound jolted her by surprise. She looked up only to see Vijay standing at the entrance. Priya had been so lost in her admiration of the watch that she did not notice Vijay, who had been observing her silently all along. On seeing him, Priya was dumbfounded and her heart skipped several beats. With panic writ large on her face, she stammered, "I was actually getting bored, so, I decided to clean up your table...When I saw this beautiful watch I just wished to see how it looked on my hand...I did not intend to steal it....."

Vijay was in no mood to listen to her rambling for his mind was now engulfed with the same odd feeling. He saw the terrified look on her face and at once decided to take advantage of her vulnerability. He bolted the door and started walking towards her. Setting aside his conscience, he wished to make the most of the moment.

Trying out his watch was not a proper thing to do and Priya knew that she was at fault. She had indeed committed a mistake and was now caught red handed. Vijay had already warned her that he was not prepared to tolerate any mistakes; however trivial they might be. She realised that he was definitely not going to let her scot-free for having pried into his personal belongings. She stood there shaking in fear; gearing up for the ordeal that was to come. However, she was determined not to retaliate. For yesterday when she had argued with him, he had slapped her and so the best recourse was to stay put.

Vijay was standing close to her and Priya's heart started pounding. She tried to evoke his pity and once again mumbled in a low voice, "Actually I was feeling very bored...I wished to involve myself in some work and decided to clean up your table... When I saw this beautiful watch I just wished to see how it looked on my hand.......I did not mean to ....."

Her pleas to prove herself innocent only fell on deaf ears. For all of a sudden, she felt his strong hands on her shoulder. Vijay had positioned himself behind her and sliding his hands into her tops, grabbed her breasts.

*Oh God! She was indeed paying a heavy price for disobedience. How many times had her mother advised her not to leave the house without a bra! She had always felt this as a burden and tried to avoid it whenever possible. She would toss it away first thing after reaching home, before attending to other chores. This morning, she was in a hurry to reach the hotel in time and hence left without bothering to wear it. She repented for having disobeyed her mother in the first place. Because she was now facing the music as Vijay was easily able to get access to her breasts.*

Fondling them, he drawled; trying to mimic her, "Actually.... I was also feeling very bored That's why.... I was standing there .... .Observing you amuse yourself with my watch."

Priya was horrified by what he was doing to her and her stomach started churning at once. She was feeling so ashamed of herself and wanted to fight back but instantly changed her mind and stuck to her resolution. Without paying any heed to his taunting, she stood there helplessly.

Seeing that she did not respond to his mocking in any way and remained impassive, he started squeezing them even harder and in a stern voice asked, "Is it fair to meddle with other's things?"

Priya started squirming in pain and tears stung her eyes. However, she continued to hang on without raising any objections for fear that she would be provoking him. While contemplating on an apt reply she could give him, she heard his cell phone buzz. She heaved a sigh of relief for he immediately abandoned her and went to attend the call.

He returned quickly only to continue his torment. This time, he treated her even more ruthlessly. He held her nipples and started pinching and twisting them brutally. "Come on, you have not answered my question yet?" he said continuing his assault on her.

Priya could no longer put up with it and she said amidst sobs, "I am sorry for wearing your watch. Please excuse me."

Vijay was actually enjoying himself giving in to his sexual pleasures. After having his fill, he finally said, "This will teach you a lesson in life not to pry into others' things."

Feigning as if he was a good employer who had just taken some disciplinary action against a worker, he said trying to console her, "You know pretty well that I am a tough person and I deal with my workmen very strictly when they do anything wrong. Being aware of this, shouldn't you be more careful?"

Priya stood there silently wiping away the incessant tears that refused to stop.

Before leaving his room, he patted her on her shoulder and said rather caringly, "Well, stop crying now and don't repeat this again, understand?"

As soon as he left the room, Priya began stroking her breasts softly to relieve herself from the lingering pain.

Vijay had taken full advantage of her ignorance by satiating his sexual urges. Only Priya was too naïve to understand that she had been a victim of sexual harassment.

In the evening, when it was time for Priya to leave, Vijay summoned her to his room. He spoke to her kindly and even enquired about her mother's health. Shoving a thousand rupee note into her hand he said, "Take her to a good doctor immediately."

Priya at first hesitated, but when he insisted, she accepted it from him without objecting further. However, she was not grateful for his act of kindness and did not thank him. She was in fact too exhausted from crying and walked home very slowly with a drooping face. On reaching home, she became sadder when she saw her mother lying in bed. As soon as her mother saw her, she made an effort to get up and sit. Looking at her glum face, she asked, "Did that fellow scold you again?"

Priya was too embarrassed to share the unpleasant experience with her mother. If her mother ever heard of this, she would be distressed and this would further affect her health. Hence Priya decided not to reveal anything to her. Suppressing all her emotions, she said, "Not really! In fact, on hearing that you are not feeling well, he gave me this thousand rupee note and asked me to take you to a good doctor." After handing over the money to her mother, she left the room immediately even without caring for her response.

For the rest of the evening Priya was busy assisting her mother in the lab in getting the various tests done. She was asked to come on the next day same time to collect the report.

That night, Priya lay wide awake, wondering what the results were going to be. All her life, she had seen her mother so active and this was the first time, she was seeing her frail and sick. She was very depressed about her mother's health and to add to this, she was also disturbed by the incidents that occurred in course of the day. Her mind was so agitated over Vijay's ill-treatment over her that she did not wish to see his face again. She lay there in the dark contemplating on the various plausible reasons she could give her mother in order to avoid going to the hotel tomorrow.

# 15

Early next morning, Priya woke up before her mother. She touched her mother's forehead and it was still hot. Using this as a pretext to escape from work, she started waking up her mother frantically. When her mother woke up she said rather gloomily, "Ma, you are running a high temperature even today and it would be better to go and see the doctor now itself." But her mother took it very lightly and said, "Let the report come first. We can then go and see the doctor then." She then tried to allay her fears, "I am going to get well soon and don't keep worrying about my health unnecessarily."

Priya was however bent on skipping work, no matter what. Once again, she began pleading with her mother, "OK then. At least allow me to stay back at home and take care of you today. I cannot leave you alone in this condition. Besides, the clothes are piling up and there are also a lot of vessels to be washed as well. I would like to help you with the household chores. Otherwise, you would further ruin your health by doing all of this yourself."

Her mother was silent and did not make any comment. While Priya was reveling in the fact that her pleas had met with success, her mother continued, "Today is the last day of the month. All the money I had at home has been spent so therefore please go and get our salary. We need it for the medical expense. Also go and meet the Chef and put in a word to him about my poor health condition and that I would be extending my leave for another two days."

Priya became dejected at once for she realised that her mother was after all correct. She was aware that her mother usually saved most of her salary in the bank and kept very less money at home. Money was required urgently to pay the medical bills and right now her mother was not in a position to go to the bank. She had no other choice but to obey her mother. *If only she had divulged the facts to her mother last night, she would have definitely not sent her for work today; whatever the exigency might have been!* She regretted for hiding the awful fact from her mother. Having no further say in the matter, she silently entered the bathroom sulking.

Reassuring herself that this was going to be her last day of work, she tried to cheer up a little. She got ready in a jiffy and left the house, earlier than usual.

Vijay was rather baffled on seeing her; for he never expected to see her again. Despite his rough manhandling of her, she had turned up for work. He was awe-struck by her strong mind and willpower to withstanding the difficulties of life. She was in fact different from the rest of the girls, he thought. "How is your mother? Did you take her to the doctor?" He asked with concern in his voice.

"No. I will be taking her this evening only after receiving the lab report." She said and made a hasty retreat.

Vijay however called her back and said, "I am actually leaving for a marriage function now and will be back only in the afternoon." Priya was happy to hear this news for she could now work peacefully without his constant vigil and railing.

It was around 11.00 am when Priya finished all her chores. Remembering her mother's request, she rushed out of the room. She met the Chef and informed him that her mother would be extending her leave by another two days. The Chef was aware that Vijay had gone out in the morning and was not around. He wished to have a small talk with her. He enquired about her mother's health and also informed her that she could feel free to contact him in case of any help. Further he asked her about her future plans. Priya told him that she would be joining college very soon and later on wished to go out for a job so that she could take good care of her mother. She was so engrossed in talking to the Chef that she was not aware of the passing time. It was during the middle of her conversation that a boy came running up to her and said, "Vijay sir is calling you immediately."

Excusing herself, Priya scurried across to his room. She saw him in a very frustrated mood rummaging something in his drawer. Frightened, she stood in front of him, wondering why he had summoned her. Looking up at her, he asked, "Where did you go ?"

"I just went to inform the Chef about my mother's leave." She said nervously.

"How many times have I told you not to leave the room, with the doors open?" He scolded.

Realising that it was her mistake, Priya remained silent.

Continuing his frantic search, he asked, "OK, now tell me where my golden watch is? I had kept it on top of the table with the intention of wearing it for the function but left in a hurry, forgetting to wear it. And now it is missing!"

Priya's heart started racing. "I don't know." She said in great fear.

Irked by her careless reply, he yelled, "What do you mean by saying I DON' T KNOW? Are you not responsible for the things in my room?" He yelled at her.

Priya's mind became totally blank all of a sudden. She could not comprehend why she was always landing up in some kind of trouble or the other. *Yesterday, she had been admiring the golden watch and today it was missing. Was he suspecting her?* Trying to convince him that she was in no way at fault, she said softly, "I did not see your watch today. In fact, I did not even go near your table."

Vijay was infuriated by her answer. "Does it have legs to walk out of this room on its own?" He asked sarcastically. "No one dares to enter my room except you. You are accountable for all the things in my room and that's why you are here. You cannot be so negligent and give me such an evasive reply. Don't try to shun off your responsibilities." He shouted angrily.

Tears fllled her eyes at his scathing remarks. She swallowed and her throat became constricted. *Surely, he was suspecting her !*

Being the last day of work in this hotel, Priya had been carrying out all her jobs meticulously to avoid any lashing from him. Probably she had got out from the wrong side of the bed today. Her leaving the room for just a few minutes has ended up in such jeopardy and here she was standing in front of him with the charge of being a thief. With quivering lips she said, "Please give me some time and I shall search the whole room thoroughly."

Relenting to her request, Vijay left the room dejected.

# 16

Priya searched the room at every nook and corner and finally gave up. An hour later, when Vijay returned after his usual rounds, Priya observed that he was in a bad temper. With a sad face, she told him that she could not find the watch anywhere.

"Do you know the value of the watch? It is worth more than three lakhs! Apart from the cost, it is our ancestral property which my father values a lot. I am now answerable to him. And I am not prepared to face the brunt of his anger." He thundered.

Priya did not respond to his outburst, for her eyes were once again brimming with tears of frustration. In *what plight had she landed herself in. On one hand her mother was sick and lying at home and here she was being held responsible for the missing watch. Oh God! How was she going to untangle herself from this dirty mess."*

Annoyed at her silence, Vijay continued his tirade, "Well, I am going to call in the police. Whoever is the culprit has to be severely dealt with. And by the way, you will be the first witness and don't be afraid to answer them if they interrogate you."

Priya's heart skipped several beats on hearing the word police. *She dreaded to even look at their faces directly; let alone answering their questions. She would hardly be able to speak in front of them and this would create suspicion in their minds about her. And what would her mother think if she came to know that she was questioned by the police for the theft of a watch. She would become heart-broken and would never be able to digest the fact!*

"Please don't call in the police. I shall search the room thoroughly once more." She pleaded.

"There is no point in wasting any more time. The room has already been checked by you and the watch could not be traced. I wish to leave it to the police to investigate further." He said harshly; unruffied by her fears.

With tears rolling down her cheeks, she begged, "Actually, I am very afraid of facing the police and won't be able to answer them properly. Hence please don't involve them in this matter. I promise to work in this hotel all my life and replace the watch to you somehow or the other."

Vijay was utterly confused and was not sure what to do. He kept staring at her terror-struck face; considering her request. Fearing a negative response from him, Priya interrupted his thoughts, "Or else, please suggest what I am supposed to do now. I shall abide by whatever you say."

Suddenly, a wicked thought passed in his mind. The golden watch seemed trivial and ceased to be of any importance to him anymore. Perhaps, God was giving him another opportunity to enjoy himself, he thought. Opportunities like this don't come every day and he wished to make the most use of it. Rational thoughts were deluding him and he was losing his mental balance. He wished to have instant gratification by fulfllling his sexual needs. In a muffied voice, he asked, "Is that so ? Are you willing to do anything I ask you to do?"

Being gullible, Priya was not aware that he was taking her for a ride. She felt relieved that he was at last condescending to her request by not involving the police in this matter and vehemently said, "Yes of course ! I promise to oblige you and shall do anything for you."

He got up swiftly and walked up to the door and bolted it

from inside. After switching off his cell phone, he proceeded towards her. Placing his hands on her shoulders, he said, lowering his voice, "Please take off your clothes and lie down on the sofa."

Priya was shocked and her face turned pale at once. *Oh God! What was he asking her to do? She had indeed promised him that she would oblige him but how could she comply with such a horrid request. How cruel of him to ask her to take off her clothes. It was like falling from the frying pan directly into the fire.* Her whole body started trembling and her insides rolled nervously. Tears suffused her eyes and her voice sank into a whisper, "What are you asking me to do? How can I do such a dirty thing?"

Seeing the shocking look on her face, Vijay said, "Well... actually you don't have to do anything. Just cooperate with me for a few minutes and I shall take care of the rest of the things."

Priya's knees started wobbling as he started unbuttoning her top. She forcibly pushed his hands away from her and with tears fiowing from her eyes, said, "I feel really ashamed and cannot do such a nasty thing."

Her non compliance was getting on his nerves. Losing his temper, he threatened her, "I demand absolute and unquestioning obedience from you. If you hesitate or refuse, you will be asking for trouble." In a violent manner, he stripped off her top and fiung it on the fioor, exposing her breasts.

Embarrassed at the humiliation, Priya covered her body with both her hands and ran to the corner of the room. Facing the wall, she started crying aloud like a child.

Vijay was empowered by an animal instinct and he was not prepared to listen to the voice of reason. His whole body was stirring with desire and he longed to touch her. And this time, he longed very badly to sink into her and bond with her. He followed her and roughly turned her around. Pulling her hands down, he said harshly, "You promised to oblige to me and there is no turning back now. Just give me your cooperation and bear with me for a while."

Folding her palms together, Priya begged amidst sobs, "Please....please let me go from here. I am very frightened."

Vijay hardly seemed to care for her pleas. In fact, her disobedience only triggered his anger even more. Lowering his voice, he warned, "Look, make things easier for your own self. Is this the way you reciprocate with kindness to me? I have saved you from the interrogation of the police and have also decided to face the brunt of my father's anger. Should you not be thankful for my generosity? Come on, stop crying now and do what you were told."

Priya stood there crying her heart out. Tears were forming rivers over her cheeks and her sobs were getting louder and louder. However, her tears and tantrums did not move him and he was in no way prepared to let her go without fulfllling his task.

Irked by her procrastination, he grabbed her breasts in a ruthless manner. Squeezing them in a savagely manner, he yelled, "Please don't test my patience." Unable to bear the pain, Priya let out a loud scream, hoping that someone would come and rescue her from this beast. But her screams were not heard by anyone and no one turned up.

*Who was going to come and help her? The workers were so scared of Vijay and always tried to keep themselves away from the area in front of his room for fear that they might bump into him. For then they will have to answer his stupid questions and listen to his reproaches. Even her mother was not around to come looking for her and was at the moment lying sick at home. She realised that she was beyond all help. No power on heaven or earth can help her right now. The best option now was to shamelessly yield to this bastard without further protesting.*

He continued mauling her breasts and Priya was writhing in pain. She was petrified and started getting feverish as her struggles against him were in vain. Too exhausted, she finally subdued a little. Bracing herself mentally for the tough ordeal that lay ahead of her, she said as her body racked in sobs, “Stop torturing me like this, I shall obey you.”

Immediately he released her and waited for her to respond. Priya hated herself for her helplessness and her total lack of power. Scowling at him, she slowly started undressing. As ordered by him, she reluctantly walked up to the sofa and lay down on it. When she saw him approaching her naked she was traumatised. She shut her eyes tight from the embarrassment and gritted her teeth allowing him to manipulate her body in whatever manner he chose.

Pinning her beneath him, he moved on top of her and started to push inside her. As he was entering her, her face contorted with severe pain. She screamed like hell as the sudden pain of his savage thrust poured through her. Slowly, he withdrew from her quivering body and rushed to the bathroom.

Ravaged with pain, Priya lay on the floor whimpering. He returned shortly and lifted her up. In a hushed voice, he started consoling her, “Priya, now stop crying. The ordeal is over.” Directing her to his private bathroom, he said, “Go and wash up.”

For the rest of the day, Priya was sitting all alone; wiping away the unrelenting tears. Vijay returned to his room only in the evening when it was time for her to leave. Handing over two covers to her, he smiled, “This is your salary for the month. Since your mother is not around, I am handing over hers also to you. Please take it home carefully and give it to her.” As Priya turned to leave, he gently tapped her shoulder and said, “Please don’t tell about this to anybody. Keep it a secret.”

As she walked back home, she kept praying to God to give her the strength to control the overwhelming emotions so as not to burst out into tears on seeing her mother. Her mother should never come to know of her wretched experience. *Oh God ! Should her vacation turn out to be such a nightmare?*

# 17

When Priya reached home, she was surprised to see her neighbour, Janaki chatting with her mother. Priya entered the house wondering why she had come here.

Janaki was in her late Fifties and like Parvathy was widowed at a very young age. However, she did not work as there was not any necessity for her to work as she received pension every month. Her only daughter Radha was settled in Mumbai and visited her once a year during the summer vacation of her son who was now studying in the third standard.

Janaki was a reserved lady and did not speak much to anybody in the neighbourhood. She led a solitary life, keeping to herself. Despite the fact that she could afford a servant maid, Janaki preferred to do all the work herself. Once she finished the household chores, she whiled away her time watching television. After a short siesta in the afternoon, she got ready for a long walk to the temple.

Janaki had great reverence for Parvathy for it was from her that she had learnt to take the calamities of life in a stride and get along with life in an uncomplaining manner. Besides, she adored Parvathy's introvert character; like her she was also aloof and never mingled with anyone in the neighbourhood. On rare occassions, when Janaki was in a very depressed mood or when she was very excited about something, she would come and meet Parvathy and share her woes and joys with her.

As soon as Priya stepped into the house, Janaki stood up to leave. Before leaving, she patted Priya on her back and said, "I had just come by here casually to inform your mother about my daughter's arrival this weekend. I was taken aback when I saw her lying in bed groaning. She was hardly able to speak and on learning that she had not eaten anything since morning, I offered her some fruit juice. She is feeling a little better now. However, I advise you to take her to the doctor immediately without any further delay. See, she is paying a heavy price for straining herself so hard; neglecting her health."

How appropriately had it been said that misfortunes do not come alone. It has turned out to be very much true in the case of Priya. For that night, when Priya took her mother to the doctor, she was in for another blow. Her mother was diagnosed with an advanced stage of *Leptospirocis* and had to be admitted to the hospital. When Priya returned home alone that too late in the night, Janaki came running to her. Priya apprised her with a sad face that her mother was hospitalised and that she had come only to collect a few things which were required by her mother during her stay in the hospital. Janaki allayed her fears and comforted her that her mother would get well soon. Further, she also volunteered to help her in any possible way.

For almost a fortnight, Priya had a hectic time. She stayed in the hospital with her mother during the nights and came home early in the morning. After attending to a few jobs at home, she prepared a light meal and went back to the hospital. She kept shunting between the hospital and home every day and was happy to note that her mother was slowly recovering. On the day of discharge, the doctor advised her mother to take good care of her health by eating nutritious food and also by not exerting herself too much as the disease could relapse any time.

After the arrival of her daughter, Janaki had plenty of time on her hand. Radha took care of the cooking and other household chores and Janaki was busy with Rahul, her grandson. She took him out frequently to the park and temples around the vicinity. On their way back home, she often stopped for a while to enquire about Parvathy and her health. While they kept talking, Rahul would go around looking for Priya. He had taken an instant liking for Priya as she entertained him with funny stories and also played with him. Many a times, when Radha did not find her son around, she would straightaway come to Priya's house in search of him.

It was after nearly a month that Parvathy went back to work at *The Venketeswara Quality Inn.* Once again, she continued to work with the same zeal and enthusiasm. However, one fine day, when she lifted a very big vessel from the stove and placed it on the floor, she felt a sharp pain in her chest. Clutching her chest, she sat down on the floor. The chef on seeing her struggling for breath knew something was not right. Immediately he called out for a boy and ordered him to take her to the nearby 24 hours Hospital. Since the pain was unbearable, Parvathy relented at once.

The doctor after examining her gave her an injection to arrest the chest pain. He concealed the fact that she had suffered a mild heart attack since he did not wish to frighten her. However, he wrote down the name of a Cardiologist and asked her to go and meet him in the evening itself. He further explained to her that since her heart was a little weak, she required immediate attention by a specialist.

Once the pain receded, Parvathy forgot all about the doctor's advice and carried on her chores as if nothing had happened to her. She lied to the chef that it was a minor indigestion problem and did not even disclose to her daughter about her visit to the doctor.

Parvathy's top most priority right now was her daughter's college admission. She wished to put her in a good college and for this was prepared to even use up her entire savings. Till such time her appointment with the Cardiologist could wait, she told herself.

Priya's results were out and she had passed out with fiying colours. While she was breaking her head as to which course to select, Radha advised her to take up Information Technology as that was the trend everywhere. She further ensured her that once she completed the course, she was sure to find a job quickly and that too with good salary.

Priya got busy in fllling up the application forms for her course. One afternoon, she returned home excitedly after submitting the forms in various colleges for admission. As soon as she stepped into her house, she felt giddy and immediately went to the bed and laid down herself. She had never before felt like this and feared if she was also affected with *Leptospirocis* just like her mother.

When her mother returned from work in the evening, Priya complained to her that she was feeling out of sorts. Her mother dispelled her fears by telling her that it must be due to her roaming about in the sun for admissions and asked her to take some rest. Later, when she offered her hot *idllis*, Priya refused to eat any of it. She told her that she was not hungry and moreover was feeling very nauseous. There was no any change in her health condition even the next morning and therefore Parvathy decided to take her to the doctor immediately for a thorough check up.

# 18

For Dr. Lakshmi, this issue at hand was mind boggling. She was at a loss of words and did not know how to reveal the shocking piece of news to Parvathy, who was sitting in front of her. When all the tests proved negative, she had requested Priya for a urine sample and stealthily got a pregnancy test done. When the results arrived, the doctor was astounded.

Well, this was nothing new for Dr. Lakshmi. She had come across similar cases even earlier in her career. Young girls who had indulged in sexual pleasures had come to her seeking help and she had clandestinely performed abortions for them. In turn, they had paid her a fat sum begging her to maintain their secret in silence. However, they were rich girls who could afford to spend money lavishly. But the fact that Priya had messed up her life was something which Dr. Lakshmi could not take with ease. In fact, it was she who had attended to Parvathy's delivery and knew Priya ever since she was born. She was also aware of the fact that Parvathy was very fond of her daughter and her entire life was centered on her. It was for her welfare and bright future that Parvathy was slogging night and day. How could Priya be so mean to her, she wondered.

After a long pause, Dr. Lakshmi finally broke the ice, "Please don't get disheartened by what I am going to say to you!" As Parvathy looked at her anxiously, she continued,

"Your daughter has spoilt her life. The report shows that she is pregnant and that the cause for the giddiness and vomiting are actually signs of morning sickness..."

Parvathy was not willing to hear any further. She felt so devastated and annoyed at the doctor's statement that she interrupted her defending her daughter, "No doctor! You must be reading somebody else's report. My daughter is very innocent and is not of that kind."

Dr. Lakshmi was sitting quietly listening to her contentions. She could indeed understand Parvathy's apprehensiveness but could do nothing about it. Seeing that Parvathy was getting very emotional, she said, "Please relax a little. Go home and talk to your daughter about this. Do not be rude or express your anger to her. Speak kindly to her and I am sure she will confess everything to you."

Parvathy stood up abruptly taking the report from her hand. As she turned to leave, Dr. Lakshmi tried to assure her, "By the way, don't worry about this. I have handled such cases before and I am here to help you out."

Parvathy walked home briskly with her heart pounding with anger and deceit. When Priya saw her mother's depressed face, she started to panic. *Was she suffering from an incurable disease? Could this be the reason for her mother's unhappiness?* Seeing that her mother was restless, Priya went in to get some water. As she handed her the glass of water, she asked, "Ma, you look so tensed. Is anything wrong?"

Parvathy gulped down the water hastily and said, "Priya, come and sit down here for a while. I wish to talk to you about something very important." Priya sat down beside her mother immediately.

Parvathy hated herself for not trusting her own daughter. But she had no other alternative and had to know the truth. Fixing a serious look with her large eyes she said, "Priya please be honest and don't hide any facts from me!" As Priya stared at her mother nervously, she continued, "Are you roaming around with any boy, without my knowledge?"

Priya was at once offended by her mother's disgusting question. She could not believe that her mother was suspecting her. "No Ma! What makes you suspect me all of a sudden?" She asked in distress. Disregarding her question, Parvathy continued, "What I mean is... Did you allow any man to touch you or come too close to you?"

Priya was appalled by her mother's blunt question. "Ma, first tell me why are you so agitated? And why do you keep asking me such unpleasant questions?"

Without beating around the bush, Parvathy pointed to the report in her hand and said, "The doctor says that your giddiness and vomiting are due to the fact that you are pregnant and this report confirms it."

Priya could not believe what she was hearing! Suddenly, the world around her started to collapse. Clutching her mother's hand she started crying, "Ma, how did I get pregnant? How did this happen to me?" Priya was so gullible that she was not aware of the facts of life. As her body racked in sobs, the truth dawned on her. *Was this the reason her mother asked her if she had let anyone come too close to her?* The mysteries of life unwrapped by itself! Priya had all along trapped her emotions about her nightmare on the last working day at the hotel; feeling too embarrassed to disclose it to her mother. But now the time has come for her to divulge everything.

With a trace of hesitation, she said rather sheepishly, "Ma, that owner Vijay under whom you asked me to work is not a good fellow. He always tried to find some fault or other with my work and used this as a pretext to abuse me. He would often pinch me and at times even slap me across my face. And when you were on leave, he went to the extent of squeezing my breasts and on the last day......"

Seething with anger, Parvathy exploded, "How could you suppress all these facts from me? Did it not occur to you that you should apprise your mother about this?"

"I had borne all his torments silently because you were sick and I did not wish to burden you with my problems for fear that you would unnecessarily start worrying and further ruin your health. Moreover, I just wanted to work there for at least one month, no matter what, so that I could make you happy with my salary. But on the last day of my work,..." Priya could not continue further with her story. Her face clouded over with a painful melancholy and her body shook with fresh sobs once again. Amidst tears, she recounted her horrendous experience to her mother. "Ma, Vijay suspected me with the stealing of his costly golden watch and wished to call in the police. He further threatened me that I would be their first target of attack. When I begged him not to involve the police in this regard, he agreed on the condition that I should cooperate with him for a while. Not having any knowledge of what he intended to do, I readily agreed. But very soon he was behaving like an animal and started ripping off my clothes and my pleas for him to stop only fell on his deaf ears. He pinned me beneath him and despite my screams did not let me free....."

Parvathy began trembling with rage as her daughter was narrating her story. Exasperated over her dauntless behaviour, she scolded, "Isn't your mother alive ? Why didn't you come out of his room at once and phone up to me, before assenting to his demands?"

Ignoring her mother's scornful tone, Priya continued, "Actually when he told me that I was answerable to the police, my mind became so disoriented. At that moment, I could only think of you and how ashamed you would be if you ever came to know that your daughter was interrogated by the police for the theft of a watch. I wanted the whole thing to be over with and ....."

"And eventually you have brought shame and disgrace to your mother, isn't it?" Parvathy asked resentfully. Priya could not answer. Her body was uncontrollably shaking and she was frightened like hell thinking about her future. *How was she going to get out of this mess she had gotten herself into?*

Parvathy too was devastated by the sudden turn of events in their lives. The truth revealed by her daughter froze the very roots of her souls existence. She sat down there contemplating about the sorrows happening in her life. *Why was God so unfair to her?* She thought.

"Ma, though I did not like to work in a hotel, I agreed to do so just to make you happy. I did even all the menial jobs, tolerated all the harassments, with the only good intention of earning some money and being of financial support to you. Unfortunately, while trying to accomplish my wish, I had landed up in trouble and was held responsible for the missing watch. Once again, not willing to tarnish your image by letting the police intervene in this case, I was forced to yield to his demand by extending my cooperation. I am now terribly sorry for bringing dishonour to you and ultimately jeopardising my life like this. What do we do now? I am too scared out of my wits; please do something to save me from this situation." Priya ranted deliriously interrupting her mother's thoughts.

Parvathy was sitting like a statue, unable to respond. For, she herself did not have an answer to her daughter's question. She was only sure of one thing! She was the main cause for everything that was happening and was responsible for ruining her daughter's life. She sat there repenting that if only she had not been so lackadaisical in nature, things would have not gone out of hand.

After her husband's death, when she was left with the responsibility of taking care of her daughter single handed, she did not wish to spread her hands in front of anybody asking for help and hence had to go out for work. All her life, she had been crazy about making money and in achieving the means to sustenance. She had no time for her daughter and had never once sat down with her for a heart to heart conversation. Nor did she think it was necessary for her to educate her about the facts of life and had brought her up in a very naïve manner. She had not been able to carry out her obligations and duties as a mother properly to the fullest. She had even been rude to her at times telling her that she was not prepared to listen to her grouches and that she had to fight the battles of life on her own.

In fact, she had committed a blunder by taking her daughter to work in that hotel. By asking her to work for Vijay, she was indeed aware that she was placing a roll of cotton near a burning fire and that her daughter was vulnerable to such mishaps. However, she had justified to herself that since she was working close to her, she would always be available in case of any trouble. But unfortunately she had fallen sick and had to be on leave when the unpleasant incident took place and her poor daughter had to endure undue suffering and misery.

Moreover, she had thought that Vijay would also be like his father. His father was a kind and good natured man who led his life with morality and principles. But her guess had been wrong and here she was completely duped. Suddenly, Parvathy's eyes widened with an immense anger and she cursed him under her breath. *That scoundrel will definitely pay for this one day.*

# 19

The room in which both the women sat contemplating resonated with shame, disgrace and a sense melancholy. Parvathy slowly got up realising that now the damage had already been done and there was now no point in crying over spilt milk. After brooding at length on what should be the next course of action, she finally came to a conclusion. She decided to meet Venketeswaran and seek justice from him.

Parvathy was racking her nerves. In fact, she was in two minds. She kept deliberating whether it was appropriate on her part to meet Venketeswaran personally about the whole situation or send someone as a representative on her behalf. So far, she had met Venkateswaran only connecting her personal problems or whenever she had to tide over a financial crisis or something. But now things were different this matter pertained his own son and Parvathy was not sure as to how he would receive the news. How would he react to it?

As usual, she decided to confide on her elderly and wise neighbour and well-wisher, Janaki. Parvathy never tried to hide any facts from her. Janaki was listening with rapt attention, to her sad story and after hearing her out fully, she asked with a frown on her face, "What are you waiting for, some kind of auspicious time or something?" As Parvathy stared at her with sorrow written all over her face; Janaki continued, "You have indeed taken the right decision in going and meeting him. Sending anybody else would be a foolish idea. You ought to maintain absolute secrecy in this regard and you cannot go about trumpeting it to everyone. Without dilly-dallying further on this issue, go and see him right away. Let us see what that old man has to say about his unruly son."

Janaki's inspiring advice gave Parvathy all the immense courage she needed at once. She was now hell-bent on carrying out her mission immediately.

# 20

As the twilight was slowly turning into darkness of the night, Priya was getting tensed. Her mother who had left in the morning had still not returned home. She wondered what could be holding her for so long. *Was she having a tiff with that man in her quest for seeking justice? Did she arouse his temper and as a result of which he had ruthlessly summoned his servants to hack her to death?* Her imaginations were soaring so high but the sudden convulsions of nausea put on a pause to her wild thoughts. She ran out of the room to vomit. Drained of all energy, she lay down on the bed and was anxiously waiting for her mother. Within a few minutes, her mother walked into the room looking very depressed and worn out. Priya's face brightened on seeing her mother back; alive.

For a moment, all her fears were replaced by an intense curiosity to know about the outcome of her meeting. However, controlling her emotions, she sat up on the bed and waited patiently for her mother to begin. Sensing her anxiety, Parvathy slowly unzipped her purse and took out the golden watch. She held it out in front of her and said, "This is for you!"

Priya was dumbfounded. She could not believe it. "Ma", she bellowed shockingly. "It is the very same golden watch that was missing. Despite my search, I was not able to trace it that day. How did it happen to come in to your hands? That fellow had heartlessly destroyed my life charging me with the theft of this watch. Please tell me how did you get this?"

Sadly, Parvathy told her daughter, "This golden watch was given to me by his father as a compensation for the evil act of his son. He said that it was a priceless gift and that he had inherited it and would have never parted it to anyone else but you. He asked me to either mortgage it or sell it and use the money exclusively for your welfare – first to do an abortion and then to educate you further."

Priya was glad to hear the news from her mother. Just a few days back, she had been admiring the golden watch and now it belonged to her. More than anything else, she would become free from the frequent bouts of giddiness and vomiting once the abortion was over. She would become normal and will be able to continue with her studies. Priya's hopes started running sky high, once again.

# 21

Janaki sat down beside her and Parvathy recounted the entire happenings of the meeting to her. After hearing her out fully, Janaki said, "This is what has been happening down the ages. The rich and the powerful continue with their atrocities and no law can stop them from doing so. It is only we the oppressed people who have to put up with their wrongs and not complain about it. For they very easily escape by covering up their misdeeds with their money. But let me tell you one thing. God is watching everything and no one can escape from His eyes. One day or the other, they are sure to meet the consequences for their actions." She paused for a while before she said, "Well, let me see the golden watch which he has given you." When Parvathy handed over the purse to her, she curiously took out the golden watch from the small pouch and started examining it closely. Finally she said, "Not bad! That man has indeed compensated you generously for the dastardly act of his son. With the value of gold mounting day after day, this golden watch would definitely fetch you several lakhs. Go and meet the doctor immediately. Fix up a date for abortion and relieve your daughter from all hardships."

Janaki's cheerful words did very little to uplift Parvathy's dismal mood. This infuriated Janaki and she screamed at her, "Why do you look so sad and down in the dumps?"

Parvathy remained glum and did not reply. Her silence was getting on Janaki's nerves and she scoffed at her, "Did you expect that Venketeswaran would get his son married to your daughter and accept her as his daughter-in-law?"

Priya who was eavesdropping their conversation, lying in bed, muffied a laugh at the way Janaki was ridiculing her mother. Parvathy did not respond to her and her scathing remarks as well. Unmindful of this, Janaki continued her tirade, "Stop being a pessimist. Learn to admire the beautiful roses and just don't keep grumbling about the thorns in the plant. It is up to us to choose between happiness and sadness. Whatever be the case, whether we are happy or sad, death is sure to lay its icy hands on all of us and we are destined to die one day or the other. Why not choose to be happy until then?"

Janaki's counselling did not alter her mood at all. Parvathy was feeling lost and low in life. She was in fact much worried about the great ordeal that lay ahead of her. Taking her daughter for an abortion was a herculean task, which she very much dreaded.

Ignoring the mild chest pain that kept lingering since afternoon Parvathy went to bed. Lying beside her daughter, who was by now having a sound sleep, she put her arm around her. Snuggling close to her, she fell asleep instantly.

# 22

After her meeting with Venketeswaran was over, Parvathy intended to first update Janaki with the news and happenings. However, she was too exhausted and hence walked home directly. Turning to her daughter, she said, “Priya, go and call Janaki. I have to apprise her about what happened today.”

Happy that she could now get a full picture about what transpired between Venketeswaran and her mother, Priya left on her errand immediately. Sitting all alone, Parvathy started musing over the events of the day....

It had indeed been another worse day of her life. She was waiting for Venketeswaran with abated breath and at last when he stepped into the hall, Parvathy got up swiftly and wished him.

Gesturing her to continue sitting, he helped himself with a chair and sat down opposite her. “How are you Parvathy? I heard from my son that you were not feeling well and were on a long leave. Are you okay now?” He asked with concern in his voice.

“I am fine, Sir.” Parvathy answered meekly.

“Well, tell me what can I do for you?”

Parvathy was feeling very embarrassed and could not find her voice. Somehow she began, slowly, “Actually, a few months back, your son had wanted me to look out for somebody who could work as a helper for him. Since my daughter was having her vacation and idling alone at home, I had requested her to work for him temporarily until I find a suitable person. Unfortunately, your son has been ill-treating her every day. However, my daughter wished to continue her job for at least a month; no matter what, so that she could please me with her salary and hence bore everything silently. On the last day of the month, he had held her responsible for a missing golden watch and threatened to call in the police. My daughter who was frightened out of her wits, and begged him not to do so and he had agreed on the condition that she extend her cooperation for a while. Being so naïve, my daughter agreed at once; not aware of his intention. This has resulted in her pregnancy and...." Words failed her and Parvathy burst into tears.

Venketeswaran was jolted out of the blue. He had been reveling in the fact that his son had turned over a new leaf and was doing well in his job. In fact, he was planning to settle his marriage shortly and here this lady just threw a bombshell at him. He sat there in silence; lost in his own private and turbulent thoughts about the shocking news he had just received. He then got up abruptly and left the place.

Within a few minutes, he returned carrying a small pouch in his hand. He walked up to the door and after making sure that no one was listening to their conversation, he said, "Parvathy, I have no words to console you. I know pretty well that you have been slogging all your life for the sake of your loving daughter. I can also understand the depth of your sad feelings and how terribly upset you must be. I am extremely sorry for the suffering undergone by your daughter on account of my son and shall surely take him to task in a befitting manner."

He then carefully took out a golden watch from the pouch and handing it over to her said in a hushed voice, "Forget this ever happened to your daughter and stop worrying. It was only due to this golden watch that your daughter had to undergo so much suffering. Now let this bring her all the happiness in life. Please accept this gift from me. I hold this very close to my heart and am now parting with this priceless gift just for your daughter. You may either mortgage or sell it and with the money, first please perform an abortion and then send her to college to pursue her studies."

Refusing to accept it, Parvathy blurted, "I did not come here for any financial compensation. I just wished to inform you that my daughter is carrying your son's baby and expect....."

Not giving her an opportunity to voice her opinion, Venketeswaran quickly interrupted her, "Please listen to me. Whenever you had come to me at the time of crisis, I have always offered you my suggestions and you had trusted my judgements and acted accordingly. I now request you to follow my advice in this matter too. Your daughter is too young to be burdened with pregnancy and the birth of a child. It would be prudent of you to take her to a good doctor and perform an abortion. She has the right to enjoy her life and this would become possible only if you educate her well. Accept this priceless gift from me and I am sure, it will bring her all the luck. It will give her the strength and courage to ferry across the ocean of life smoothly."

Parvathy was indeed aware that his feelings for her were genuine and that he was speaking from his heart. She did not retort further and stood there wiping away here tears. Venketeswaran forcibly took the purse from her hand and dropped the pouch into it. Returning it to her, he said, "Now, please control your emotions. If any of the servants see you crying, they would cook up some cock and bull story and spread unnecessary rumors."

Taking the hint and having no other option, Parvathy dragged her feet towards the door with a disturbed mind.

The arrival of Priya accompanied by Janaki intruded her thoughts and she at once came out of her reverie......

# 23

Radha stretched out her hand to turn off the alarm so that she could continue sleeping for some more time. But sleep evaded her for there was great hue and cry outside her house. A loud shrieking noise made her almost jump out of bed. She looked out of the window to find out the cause of commotion.

Radha was stunned when she saw her mother trying in vain to console Priya, who looked so traumatised and terrified. Priya let out another sharp cry of pain and suspecting something untoward must have happened, Radha rushed out of the house...It was early in the morning and Priya was disturbed by a bout of vomiting. She was surprised to see her mother lying so close to her. Gingerly, she lifted her hand and after placing it on the pillow, ran to the bathroom. Five minutes later, she came and sat down on the bed; tired and exhausted. She decided to wake up her mother and inform her that she was feeling very sick and out of sorts. She prodded her to get up, but her mother did not respond. She rocked her back and forth and saw that her mother was lying still like a log of wood. "Ma, Ma, Ma!" she screamed on the top of her voice. But her mother showed no sign of movement.

Her mother was an early riser and even a feeble noise would startle her out of a deep slumber. Priya wondered, why her mother was not coming to help and assist her when she was vomiting and was anxious as to why she was not waking up now. She peeped out of the window and was glad to note that Janaki was already up. She was making *rangoli* designs in front of her house with rice fiour, which was her usual ritual flrst thing in the morning.

Priya scurried across to meet her, with her heart beating frantically. On seeing Priya's worried face, Janaki immediately abandoned her work and accompanied her. Parvathy's face was colorless and Janaki at once smelt something flshy. She took her hand and felt her pulse. Hugging Priya close to her, she cried, "Your mother has left all of us. Probably she would have suffered a massive heart attack last night. She had all along been feeling guilty that she was the cause for ruining your life. She died more from depression and shock."

Priya could not believe what she was hearing. She shrieked in great horror, running about her house. On hearing her ear shattering screams, the neighbours started gathering in front of her house. However much they tried, they were unable to bring Priya under control....Radha was moved by her heart rending cries. She had a tough time trying to calm and console her. She endeavored to bring her out of the initial shock by pointing out that the worst has happened and she had to accept the fact as nothing could be done about it. Further, it was a grueling task for Radha in getting her to attend to the activities in connection with the last rites of her mother.

# 24

A week had passed after her mother's death and Priya continued to be in a grieving mood. She mourned her mother's death by crying all the time. Very often, she would isolate herself and start weeping thinking of her mother until she was drained of energy.

Her parents had eloped with each other, deserting their families. Years later after her father's death when her mother had tried to unite with her family members, they had turned their backs on her by disowning her. Since then her mother had led an independent life. Priya had never had an opportunity to meet any of her relatives. Even now, it was the neighbours who had come forward to offer timely succor to her. This being the case, Priya was now worried as to how she was going to lead a life of solitude in this house. She did not let Janaki go to her house and requested her to stay with her. Janaki kept allaying her fears by reassuring her that she would be available to her anytime and that she could consider her like her own mother.

Radha was busy packing up her bags and baggage's. In another couple of days, she was planning to return to Mumbai as her son's vacations were coming to an end. This time, she had not been able to enjoy with her mother for she had been away; giving company to Priya who refused to let her go. After having her breakfast, Radha went to meet her mother.

The door was wide open and Priya was sitting on the bed all alone, sobbing. Holding a small glass frame photograph of a God she was crying, "I offered my prayers daily in front of you. Why did you behave so unfairly with me? Why did you forsake me like this? My mother meant the whole world to me. How could you be so cruel and stone hearted?" Turning hysterical all of a sudden, she flung the photo across the room yelling, "From this moment on, you cease to exist in my life anymore!"

Radha was rather irked by this insane behaviour of hers. She picked up the shattered glass pieces and dropped them into the dustbin. After clearing up the mess, she admonished her, "That's enough Priya! It is now about time for you to come out of your mourning. By grumbling like this or expressing your anger, your mother is not going to come back. You are a young girl and have got the whole life ahead of you. Don't let your hopes falter and fall apart. I know it is a deep loss to you. But you have to rise above this deep loss and accept the changes with grace and courage."

Priya held Radha's hands and amidst tears said, "My mother has left me all alone in this world and gone. I am not sure how my future is going to be. There is no one I can call my own. I feel like an orphan......"

Engulfed by a wave of pity, Radha was quick to retort, "You are not an orphan. We are all here for you. If you are willing, you can come along with me to Mumbai. I shall take care of you."

Janaki who just stepped out of the bathroom butted in, "How can that be possible? Your husband will not agree to that?"

Surprised to see that her mother was coming out of the bathroom after having a bath, Radha at once quipped, "My husband will abide by whatever I say. He is working as a driver in a transport company and keeps travelling most of the time. He visits me once a week and sometimes, he is away even for a month. He will not say anything against my decision."

Glad to hear that her daughter was evincing keen interest in Priya and was volunteering to help her, Janaki said, "In that case, I shall take Priya to the doctor today itself and get the abortion done. You can then take her along with you."

Swiftly, Radha got up and taking Priya aside asked her, "Are you sure you want to get this abortion done? I would suggest that you drop the idea. Just a few minutes back, you were weeping that there is no one in this world that you can call your own. The baby growing inside your womb is after all your child too. All this morning sickness you are suffering now will pass away soon and within a few months, you will have a cute baby in your hands – your bundle of joy. The baby will bring a new meaning into your life. Why do you want to kill a baby unnecessarily for no fault of it and incur a sin?"

Priya was in fact confused not sure of anything right now. The absence of her mother left a big lacuna in her life. She was really desperate and right now her mind was totally blank. She felt like a person who was blind folded and left all alone in a forest. Radha was taking quick decisions on her behalf and Priya timidly nodded her head to everything she said. After all she had no idea of how to lead her life and implicity obeyed Radha by entrusting her life into her hands. Gathering all her inner strength she took a great plunge and accompanied Radha to Mumbai.

# 25

The decision Radha had taken of bringing Priya along with her to Mumbai was on an impulse; swept by a wave of sympathy. However, Radha never once regretted her decision for Priya never gave room for it. True to her words, Radha had been taking care of Priya with love and affection and in return Priya tried to be of great help to her. Radha was working as a clerk in an Arts College and was forced to leave her son Rahul in a crèche when she was away at work. After Priya's arrival, there was no necessity for that as she was very loving and took good care of Rahul. She also took the responsibility of all the household chores on her shoulders and kept herself busy the whole day thus giving Radha some time to relax.

In order to cheer her up, Radha took her to the movies and frequent outings. But however much she tried, she was unable to bring Priya out of her sorrow. The troubled and melancholy expression continued to remain on her face.

Priya was nearing her last leg of pregnancy and one evening when Radha returned from work, she complained of unbearable labor pain. Radha rushed her to the hospital and within two hours Priya gave birth to a boy baby. On seeing her son, Priya was thrilled. She named him Vikram and as predicted by Radha, Vikram, turned out to be the apple of her eyes and brought smile and happiness on her face. Vikram grew up very fast and it was now time to put him in a school.

Though Radha was facing financial constraints, she never complained about it to anybody. She resolved her crisis by simply foregoing her little pleasures like having refreshing juices from the canteen, taking an auto or buying new saris. Now, with the addition of another member in the family, Radha was feeling the pinch for money.

Of late, she was forced to borrow money from her colleagues; especially her new boss, Somnath, he was in his mid-thirty's, and was the new art Director. He had joined the college recently. He was a kind-hearted gentleman and had a gift of utmost empathy for others. By simply looking into the eyes of a person, he could tell what kind mood he was in. Every day, when Radha went to meet him immediately on his arrival, carrying his letters, he would enquire if everything was okay with her and Radha would nod with a smile. On days when he found her in low spirits, he would ask her if anything was wrong. In the beginning, Radha had lied to him that she was fine. Slowly, learning about his benevolent nature, she shared her financial problems with him and he would readily offer his help.

Somnath was very bold and had a heart of gold. He confronted the top officials regarding the college management and gradually brought about improvements in the functioning and style of the Arts Department. One area he found that was neglected was the nude model study classes. To Somnath, human anatomy played an important aspect of training of an artist. For these, nude model study classes formed the very basic teaching for the students of art study. He noticed that a few who volunteered for this job were from the low strata of society and did not take up this job seriously. They came for work at their own whims and fancies and left after working for just a short duration.

In order to encourage people to come forward for nude modeling, Somnath approached the management to enhance their pay and also extend a few benefits to them. His efforts paid off and met with success and one day when Radha went to him with his letters, he said, "If you know any lady willing to work as a nude model, please let me know. I shall pay her a good salary and also give her free accommodation." After informing him that she was not aware of any such person, Radha turned out leave. It was only after reaching her table that it suddenly struck her and she thought, *would Priya be interested in such a job? After all, Somnath was a courteous and respectable man. The students of this college were also very disciplined and well-mannered. Priya would surely not have any problems and she would be safe and sound working here. If only she could convince her somehow to take up this job, she would be relieved from all her financial burdens.* Radha was now determined to seize the opportunity, no matter what!

# 26

For the rest of the day, Radha kept deliberating on this subject. She in fact had been responsible for bringing Priya out of her depression. Further, by advising her to give birth to her child, she had also brought meaning into her life. Like a mother bird, she had been protective and had taken care of her without any complains for three years now. Now that her wings were stronger, it was time to let her fly on her own and venture out into better pastures. She did not wish to be the protective mother bird all her life. But how was she going to talk to Priya about this, without offending her? Setting aside all her doubts and speculations, she decided to give it a try. Afterall, a trial costs nothing.

It was late in the night, when Radha opened up the topic with Priya. Without beating about the bush, she told her point blank, "Priya, a new Art Director has joined our college. He is so generous and helps everyone who approaches him with their problems. I myself have borrowed money from him several times. Today, he requested me to find a lady who would be willing to pose as a model for his art students. All that she will be required to do is to sit still for a few hours thus enabling the students to sketch her. And for this, he said he would be paying Rs.10,000 as salary and also promised to offer free accommodation to her. If you are interested, I can recommend that job for you."

Priya was stumped and became speechless. For her, it seemed as though Radha was reading her mind for she was echoing her own thoughts.

Today, for the first time in three years, Priya felt that she could not continue living here for long. And it was all due to Rahul. Ever since the birth of Vikram, Rahul had been behaving indifferently with her. He did not like the new inclusion in the family and could not bear to see them together. Whenever Priya was not around, he would act violently by either pinching or hitting Vikram for no reason at all. He would then make haste from there, leaving Vikram to cry out loud. Priya had of course caught him red handed many a times, but she had never once yelled at him. In fact, she did not wish to be ungrateful to Radha by ill-treating her son when she was away. A week back, Radha had presented Vikram with a tricycle on his third birthday. Rahul was spiked with jealousy whenever he saw Vikram riding his tricycle. When no one was watching, Rahul would shove him off his tricycle and sit on it. Despite his tantrums, Vikram would happily come around to it; provoking him. This morning, Vikram had been very stubborn and refused to let go the tricycle by holding the handle bars in a strong grip. Infuriated about this, Rahul bit his hand that left an imprint of his teeth on the little ones flesh. On hearing the wild shrieks of her son, Priya came running to the room. Her mind was so upset at the unruly behaviour of Rahul which was becoming bad to worse day by day. Suppressing her anger, she lifted Vikram and walked away from the scene of dispute, without as much as a word to Rahul. As Priya was nursing his wound she thought that it was not possible for her to continue living here for long. When an opportune moment arrived, perhaps she had to make a move from here.

Now, Radha was herself asking her if she was interested to go out for a job. The salary was indeed attractive and the free accommodation was an added bonus. She would be able to lead an independent life and also bring up her son in a comfortable manner. Concealing her excitement of starting life afresh with her loving son, she said without second thoughts, "If you insist and want me to go for this job, I shall definitely go."

Radha suddenly fell silent and got into one of her brooding moods. For no reason, she was at once filled with an acute sense of guilt. Was it fair on her part to send Priya for such a job? Then she reassured herself that no harm would come to Priya. After all, she was going to be in safe hands with Somnath who was a man with a heart of gold. Seeing that Radha was seriously preoccupied with some thoughts, Priya said, "You look worried and seem to be deeply in some thought. Is anything wrong?"

"Yes Priya. You are indeed right. What I told you was only one side of the picture; I was just wondering how to reveal the other side of the picture to you. Actually....while posing, you will have to take off your clothes as this is for nude modeling and that's why I was feeling rather reticent to disclose it to you." On hearing this, Priya's heart almost stopped a beat and her spirits came gliding down. She would die of embarrassment posing nude in front of the students, she thought. She did not express her opinion to Radha at once for fear that she would be annoying her. However, Radha was quick to notice the tension and hesitation on her face and she chipped in, "Don't bother Priya. Just forget this. I had already informed the Art Director that I am not aware of any such person." Before leaving she said, stifling a yawn, "In case you don't have any reservations and wish to do this kind of service to the art students, please feel free to tell me tomorrow morning. I shall then speak to my boss about it."

Radha was indeed glad that she was successful in divulging the facts to Priya. The ball was now in her court and it was up to her to decide. And as for the decision Priya was going to take, she did not care.

# 27

Priya kept pondering over the offer and breaking her head whether to go or not for the job of nude modeling. At first she was traumatised but as she kept mulling over it, she thought, *why not*. She considered Radha as her Godmother and respected her views and suggestions. She blindly abided by all her decisions without caring for the repercussions of her actions. And now, it was Radha herself advising her to take up this job. She referred to it as a service to the students of art and so perhaps she could give it a try. She would thus stop being a burden on Radha. Suddenly, her inner voice screamed back at her, "Aren't you ashamed to sit bare bodied in front of so many people?" And sadly she justified it to her conscience. *"Not really! After all I do have a horrible experience in my past of taking off my clothes. Moreover, nothing matters to me anymore; especially after my mother passing away. I have become immune to any feelings and am devoid of all emotions. I have come to that point in my life, when being right or wrong does not make much difference any more. Well, I do feel ashamed to take up this job but then beggars cannot be choosers. I do not have the luxury to make choices. Like a street dog, I have to rest happy with the crumbs of bread that is thrown at m !"* It took her the whole night to work up the courage to announce her decision to Radha.

While timidly giving her consent to Radha early next morning, she said, "I am worried about what the around would say if they ever found out that I am working as a nude model." Radha was elated that Priya had agreed to go for the job. Her heart went out to her immediately and blessing her wholeheartedly, she restored her confidence, "Priya, this is Mumbai and not Chennai. Here people are too busy with their own lives and have got no time for prying into other people's lives. No one is going to come and ask you what you do for a living. And by the way, when you are in need of money, this world is not going to come and help you but you have to help yourself. As long as you have money and portray yourself as being rich, people will respect you and they will never bother to ask how you are making that money." Priya was all set now.

Very eager to please her boss, Radha took Priya to the college on the same day. Requesting he to wait outside, Radha went in. Somnath was talking on the phone and he gestured with his hand for her to sit. Radha waited patiently for him to finish his conversation and then said rather enthusiastically, "Sir, yesterday, you had asked me if I knew anybody who would be interested to do nude modeling. I have brought a lady along with me today. She was widowed soon after her marriage and is now living with her three year old son. She is willing to do this job in order to bring up her son comfortably."

"Please ask her to see me." He said.

Within a few seconds, Priya nervously entered the room. As his eyes fell on her, Somnath was stunned. She was young and beautiful and never before had anyone of her age come forward for such a kind of job. *She must be in dire need of money to volunteer for being a nude model*, he thought; smitten with awe. Looking at her, he asked, "Do you know the nature of job you will be required to do here?"

"Yes, sir." Priya slowly nodded.

Somnath noticed that her hands were trembling. He then said, "You look so terrified. Are you sure you can handle this job?"

Immediately putting on a bold front she maintained her countenance, Priya assured him that she could indeed do this job.

"Well, you ought to consider this as a service you will be doing to the students of the art stream of this college. You will depict a work of art and my students will be learning and developing their skills by sketching your body day after day. If you feel at ease in doing this job, you are welcome to join us at your convenience."

Timidly, Priya expressed her readiness to come for work the next day itself. Radha who was so far standing beside her quietly, turned to leave after thanking him profusely and Priya silently followed her. On seeing that Priya's eyes were glistening with tears, Radha assuaged her fears, "Many nude models who worked here before had also felt this job to be very disgusting and humiliating in the beginning. But with the passage of time, they picked up courage and confidence and became very cool about it." Priya did not respond to her and continued to be grim and taciturn; for words failed her. All of a sudden she broke down thinking of her mother. *If only she was alive, there would be no necessity for her to stoop so low for making a living.*

# 28

The next day when Priya went to report to him, Somnath greeted her with a warm smile. He got up at once to show her the cabin where she will have to be seated when she was not doing her job of posing. For the first two days, Priya was sitting idle with nothing to do. It was on the third day that Somnath came to her cabin and asked her to get ready for a posing session. *This was going to be another nightmare*, she thought as she kept walking behind him with her heart beating rapidly. Somnath entered a big hall but Priya stopped abruptly as her eyes fell on the words "*Entry Restricted*" on the door. Realising that Priya had not followed him, Somnath popped his head out and requested her to come in. Once she was in, he immediately bolted the door and proceeded towards the stage in front of the hall.

Priya was shocked and scared to all of a sudden see what was before her. There were about thirty students, both boys and girls sitting there and everyone's eyes were on her. The serious looks on their faces and the pin drop silence prevailing in the room frightened her even more. All of them were sitting in front of a drawing board, ready with a pencil to commence their drawing.

Pointing to a raised platform at the center of the stage, Somnath said, "Priya, you will now have to disrobe and climb on to that platform." When Priya caught a glimpse of a crystal chandelier illuminating the platform brightly, her hands turned cold. She could feel the pressure building up inside her and the trickling streams of perspiration down her spine. For a moment, she stood there vacillating. Apart from being ashamed, she was also filled with guilt at what she was about to do.

*The face of Vikram loomed large in front of her. It was she who had brought him into this world. She was the one and only person who had to protect her son. She did not want him to grow in poverty or lead a horrible life. Gathering all her inner strength, she tried to compromise with her plight and make the best out of a bad situation.*

As if aware of her mental tribulations, Somnath said in a calm and reassuring voice, "Please take a few deep breaths and relax a little. Imagine that you are doing a service and all these students are going to benefit out of this." His inspiring words emboldened her and all of a sudden she could feel a drastic change from within. Shivering, she slowly started taking off her clothes. Somnath, then started giving her instructions to pose and Priya complied with him. Finally, satisfied with her posture, he said, "That's fine now, please remain still until I tell you." Turning to his students, he commanded, "You may now start sketching her and the time allotted for this is half an hour."

After ten minutes, Priya realised that her body had turned numb. She also suffered from acute muscle cramps. However enduring the pain, she continued sitting; eagerly waiting for his orders. Half-an-hour later, Somnath told his students to stop drawing. Going up to Priya with a thumb's up sign he said, "Good job done. You may go to the adjoining room and get into your clothes." Picking up her clothes, Priya ran towards the dressing room.

Once inside the room, Priya heaved a sigh of relief. *She was alive! She did not die of embarrassment! Perhaps she could make it!* After wearing her dress, she stood there relaxing her muscles and stretching herself to feel comfortable.

Somnath was busy inspecting the works of his students and offering them his comments on their works. After disposing them off for their next class, he called out for Priya. Priya approached him with shyness; too exhausted and drained out of energy. Aware that it was the first time that Priya was doing this kind of a job, he said, "I know that it would have been a hell of an experience for you today. Well...as I said earlier, don't belittle any job that you do and learn to derive a sense of satisfaction in whatever you are doing."

Over time with regular practice, Priya got over the body aches and pains. She was easily able to pose for many hours during the day. She would conveniently pick up a point on the wall in front of her and keep staring at it as if she were practicing yoga or meditation. With the passing of each day, Priya became more and more confident of handling this job. Eventually, her inhibitions, shame and embarrassment that she was initially feeling had gone. These feelings were replaced with a sense of fulfillment and satisfaction in whatever she was doing.

The students studying art also respected her and were kind to her. In fact, they vied with each other to get a chance to talk to her during breaks or after the class. Many of them even shared their personal problems with her. On festive occasions, she was showered with a lot of gifts.

As envisioned by her, there was no dearth of money and she was able to bring up Vikram in a luxurious way. One fine day, she moved out from Radha's apartment after thanking her profusely for all the kindness in giving her a new lease of life.

# 29

The wheel of time moved very fast and Vikram soon grew up to be a young lad. He was now doing his final year in Information Technology. Over the years, Priya's fears, depression and loneliness were fully wiped away. However, apart from her mother, she continued to miss two other people who had been of great help to her in her life. The first was Radha who had left Mumbai for good a few years back and settled down in her husband's home town in *Kanchipuram* along with her mother who was now old and sick. She was now assisting her husband in running his travel agency. The other person was Somnath, who had always been very kind and understanding towards her; he retired from his services a few months ago. His place was taken over by Rita. Rita was a young and energetic lady who displayed great enthusiasm in her work. Not satisfied with the simple sitting and reclining poses, she requested Priya to do some twisting poses as well. Priya was thirty eight years old now and her age was now telling upon her health. Unlike before, she was finding it difficult to sit for long hours for the posing sessions. However, she did not give up and tried her best to satisfy Rita and be in her good books.

Every evening, when Vikram returned from College, he was irked to hear his mother always grumble about her body aches. One day, seeing her sprawling on the floor, stretching out her hands and legs; groaning in pain, he asked her in a jovial way, "What type of job are you doing in the college? Hope you are not working as a coolie or something?" Priya was silent and did not answer that.

*When Vikram was a child, he had once asked her about the job she was doing and Priya had simply told him that she was working as an Assistant for an artist in the Art department of a college. Vikram had not understood then but however, he had never probed into it further.*

Priya silently took the bottle of pain killer and was about to pop one into her mouth, when Vikram grabbed it from her hand yelling, "Haven't I told you several times not to take these pain killers? Aren't you aware that by regularly using these tablets it will affect your health in the long run?" Failing to appreciate her son's concern for her, Priya said rather curtly, "I am getting old day by day and I just cannot do without these pills from now on."

"Why not? You can deflnitely do without them." Vikram said grinning. As Priya looked up at him not able to comprehend what he was saying, he said, "Resign your job and take rest at home. There is no need for you to go for work henceforth. Just cook for the two of us, watch television and read your favorite magazines."

Priya was wondering why her son was behaving in a very queer manner when Vikram continued, "During the campus interview today, I have been selected for a job in a very reputed IT company. They are offering me a salary of Forty Thousand rupees a month." Reveling in the great news, Priya was staring at him in disbelief; that is when Vikram further said, "But the posting is in Chennai and we will have to move out from here. On learning that my mother tongue is *Tamil*, they asked me if I was prepared to work in Chennai and I readily agreed."

At once, Priya's spirits that were soaring high came falling down and she became very sad. She had hated Chennai to the core and did not wish to go back ever to that dreadful city. Bad memories fiooded her mind. She felt that by returning to Chennai she would be treading into dangerous waters for there was a chance that she might bump into the man who had ruined her life. However, reserving her fears and doubts to herself, she accompanied her son to Chennai. Because, if she refused, she would owe an explanation to her son which was plausible, and she was not willing to tell him anything.

# 30

Hell had indeed broken loose; for Priya's fears had really turned out to be true. Vijay had audaciously accompanied Vikram to her house. *What if he found out that Vikram happened to be his son? What if he tried to influence him and snatch him away from her?* The time had at last come for her to open Pandora 's Box of secrets and divulge the truth to her son. *There was no point in keeping him in the dark further more. She will have to warn him not to get too close to that cruel fellow.* Just as Priya was lost in these thoughts a loud bang at the door brought Priya out of her fearful trance, back into reality...

Making a concentrated effort to put the past out of her mind, Priya stood up and went to open the door. Vikram was standing there with a bandage on his forehead. He walked in silently without acknowledging her presence. After placing the bag containing her tiffin in the kitchen, he straightaway went to bed. The fact that she was responsible for his injury pained her heart. Sitting beside him, she apologized, "Vikram, I am very sorry for my rough behaviour son ...."

Vikram was in no mood to compromise with his mother. He was still furious with her. Interrupting her he said rather harshly, "Ma, please try to control your anger first. I am telling this for your own good because anger will surely destroy your health. You behaved in a very cold, ruthless and unfeeling manner by asking that elderly man to leave, despite the fact that I had invited him home. He is a true friend of mine and the love he has for me is unparalleled. I have been a loner; lapsed into my cocoon, in my childhood, adolescence and early youth but after my friendship with him I have changed completely and have started reaching out to people. How can I break that friendship? Parting from him is a sorrowful thing to me."

"Vikram, before saying anything further will you please listen to me patiently for a while? I have got to talk to you about something very important. Before storming out of the house, you told me that you did not wish to make friends with your peer group because they were all of the type for whom life is having fun at the cost of others' misery. Vijay, your so called best friend is also such a kind of person!"

"Do you know him already?" Vikram asked inquisitively.

"Yes!" Priya said and started narrating her sordid story.

"Many years back, my mother was working at *The Venketeswara Quality Inn.* During my twelfth standard summer vacation, she requested me to work as a helper for Vijay, who had just then taken over the management of the hotel from his father. He had great fun at my cost. I had been a victim of repeated sexual harassment under his hands and one fine day, taking advantage of the fact that my mother was on sick leave, he charged me with the theft of a golden watch and threatened to call on the police. I was scared out of my wits, and I begged for his mercy and he yielded assent on the condition that I oblige him in whatever way he wants. And you were the result of the games he played with me. Later, when my mother went to meet his father seeking justice, the old man had sent her away with this golden watch as a compensation for the atrocities committed by his son; advising her to sell or mortgage it and perform an abortion for me clandestinely. My mother returned home too depressed and the next day she died of a heart attack. Alone in this world bereft of any kith and kin, I decided to give birth to you so that I could have somebody to call of my own. Come what may, I was intent upon raising you in a comfortable way and for this I did not even deter to stoop low in life and accepted the job of posing as a nude Model in the Arts College. In fact, I was not interested to come down to Chennai for fear of stumbling upon this man one day or the other. And all my fears have turned out to be true and I am now terrified that he will use his influence and snatch you away from me once he learns that you happen to be his son. That's why I had been so angry and upset with you and asked you to sever all your ties with him."

# 31

Vikram was bewildered and was crucified mentally. He could not believe what he was hearing and was unable to take it. He was rather shattered by the news; more so because of the fact that his mother had been deluding him all these years into believing that his father had died the instant he was born. After a long silence he said, "Ma, your fears are unwarranted. I am not a child anymore for anyone to use his influence and usurp me from you. Well, since you insist that I keep away from him, I promise not to meet him again!"

The promise Vikram had made to his mother, however was not from the bottom of his heart. *What a twist of fate*, he thought lying on his bed. The man whom he had befriended and revered turned out to be his own father! And his mother here is telling him not to meet his father again. He became very depressed and started feeling terribly isolated.

Early next morning, Priya woke her son up with a cup of hot coffee. As he was sipping the coffee, Priya touched the bandaged area of his forehead and Vikram flinched in pain. "Does it hurt even now?" She asked kindly, feeling sorry for him. Vikram shook his head as if to saying no. Noting that his mother was in a relaxed mood, he decided to open out his heart to her irrespective of the consequences. All his pent-up emotions surged forth at once.

"Ma, I never knew that you could turn out to be so wild all of a sudden. That poor man has been through hell losing all of his family. He just had come all the way to seek forgiveness from you. I personally feel that it was not appropriate on your part to have turned him out so rudely. The right thing would have been to forgive him. Everyone has their own faults and nobody is perfect in this world. After all, in the end, it is affection and love which is greater than perfection...." Vikram stopped abruptly when he saw his mother's face radiating with anger. "Vikram, will you please stop talking about him?" She said very irate. Vikram was determined to placate her anger towards his father and hence continued, "I know he has tormented you enough. But why don't you consider everything as a blessing in disguise? I would not have come into your life but for him. God had already punished him for his misbehavior then why don't you pardon him now after all these years? In fact, by forgiving him, you are only doing yourself good. You will feel much better. Hatred and revenge will only hurt you and increase your wound further. Do good things and good things will happen and everything will get better."

Ignoring his advice, Priya said with a frowning face, "Vikram, please don't lecture me. I know what I am doing. I am not willing to forgive him. Not in this lifetime! It was due to that wretched fellow, that I lost my mother and all my dreams in life got shattered. How can I forget all that?"

"Well, I can understand your feelings and how much aggrieved you must have been, then when you lost your mother. But were you not responsible for all the things that happened to you? Though your life was not going right, were you not going right? Ultimately, God has not let you down, has he? Things are getting straightened out now. Perhaps everything happened for a reason. Please stop brooding over the past and start living in the present. Why don't you change your mind and forgive him, at least for my sake?"

Grabbing the empty cup and saucer from his hand, Priya left the place witha huff. She did not like the way Vikram was speaking in favor of Vijay. Seeing that Vikram was silently following her, Priya yelled back at him,"Vikram, I am not willing to hear anything further regarding this subject."

"Ma, please stop screaming at me like this. All along, I have seen you only as a humble person with the patience of a saint. Your face looks ugly when you shout on the top of your voice like this."

Not giving heed to his remarks, Priya said with a stern expression, "Vikram, remember you promised me! Don't ever evade from this. Please be honest and keep up your word. Never go and see that man again. Is that clear?"

Vikram gave a silent nod. Disappointed that his mother was so obstinate and that he could do nothing to change her mind, he said in a rather frustrated voice, "Ma, but you have never been honest with me all my life. You say, you detest that man and that you are not willing to forgive him forever. However, you had treasured his golden watch as a priceless gift all your life. You did not even wish to part with it even to give me except on my birthdays. And all along you have been lying to me that I did not have a father. Since you love me so much and keep telling me that I am the apple of your eye, I bet you would have been thinking of him all along; willingly or unwillingly, almost every day of your life whenever you see me, as he is my father."

Priya lowered her head and bit her lip to suppress a smile that might have crossed her face. For a moment, she was surprised and wondered if it was her little son who was talking like this. She realised at that instant that Vikram had indeed become matured over the years. In fact, he was actually right. For Vikram was as tall and handsome like his father and resembled him to a great extent so much so that she could not help thinking of Vijay despite her aversion towards him. But how could she openly accept this fact? She was tongue-tied and did not retort further.

Vikram was quick to notice a quiver of smile escape fromhis mother's lips. Happy that he was at least able to cajole his mother into a smile, he left the room; now confident that someday in the distant future, perhaps he would be able to bring his parents together.

As Priya was preparing breakfast, she thought that it had indeed been rightly said that *ignorance is bliss.* All these years, she had kept Vikram in the dark and her life had been going on smoothly. Now that Vikram was aware of the truth, he was pointing a finger at her and accusing her. She pondered at length whether it was correct on her part to dissuade her son from meeting his own father. While she hated Vijay to the core, was it fair to think that Vikram should also harbor such feelings and abhor him? Warning bells started ringing in her mind. It was clear that Vikram adored his father and was supportive of him. One day or the other, both father and son might get together. She had to be mentally prepared and gear up herself if such a situation arises. *If only she had not come down to Chennai, life would have continued to be smooth for me!* she thought.

# 32

Vijay kept staring at the photo for a long time. He was rotating it in all possible directions and continued to admire it. He then placed it on the table and heaved a sigh. Vijay had been in a sad mood for the past few days. His visit to Priya's house had not resolved his problem at all. Ever since that day when Vikram had shown the golden watch to him and told him that it belonged to his father who was no more and that his mother treasured it as a priceless gift, Vijay had lost his sleep. He had noticed the name "Venketeswaran" embossed on it and was curious to know who exactly was Vikram's father.

It pained his heart that Priya was not even willing to see his face and had ordered him out. He chuckled suddenly on the fact that despite her railing, Vikram was innocently coaxing him to have the hot *pakodas* and how shamelessly he was gorging on them; unaffected by her angry outbursts. While he had created a tornado in her mind by his mere presence, he was calmly relishing the *pakodas* all the while talking to Vikram. That is how he had always felt in front of her-cool, relaxed and peaceful. From the moment, his eyes fell on her; he had had a crush on her. He was in fact carried away by her timidity and lovely face that seemed frightened. Suddenly, his mind went back to the dreadful day when he had held her responsible for stealing the golden watch........

Everything had been in his favour on that fateful day. He had gone wild with greed and wanted very badly to touch and fondle her. The missing watch had just been a timely pretext for him. Overcome by an animal instinct, he had used her to fulfill his sexual desires. However, that night, when he returned home he was shocked beyond words, when he saw the golden watch on his father's hand. "How did this land up on your hand?" He asked with his heart in his mouth. His father who was not aware of his son's mental turmoil, coolly replied, "This morning, while I was on my way to the marriage function, I came to the hotel to pick you up. I was waiting in your room when all of a sudden my eyes fell on the golden watch. One of the boys informed me that you had already left for the marriage and hence I decided to wear it for the function." Giving the watch back to him he said, "Keep it safely. Don't leave it around carelessly in this manner."

The next day, he was keenly waiting for Priya in order to seek forgiveness from her. But there was no sign of her or her mother. And when she did not turn up on the next day or the day after, he knew for sure that she had quit her job. Ever since then, he had been suffering from an acute sense of guilt for having wronged an innocent girl.

Parvathy recovered soon after and had joined work shortly thereafter. She came to his room on the very first day she joined and ignorant of whatever had happened between him and her daughter during her absence, she apologised that her daughter was not interested in the job and hence had discontinued. Vijay quietly nodded his head; glad that she did not mention anything about his dastardly act. After that, Vijay had tried to keep himself as far away as possible from her.

A few months later, one afternoon, he saw Parvathy getting down from an auto in front of his house. She looked so run-down and depressed and smelling that something was fishy, Vijay escaped to the adjoining room to eavesdrop the conversation between Parvathy and his father. "Your son has misbehaved with my innocent daughter, blaming her for stealing a golden watch. As a result of this my daughter is now pregnant....." Parvathy was crying her heart out in front of his father. It was with great difficulty that his father was able to placate her anger and appease her. It was then that he had given Parvathy the golden watch as a compensation for his immoral act and requested her to sell it and use the money to abort the baby and for her education.

Immediately after seeing Parvathy off, he had walked in angrily and confronted his son for his sinful act and the disgrace he had brought to him. Very soon, he settled his marriage with Swathi, his friend's daughter without even caring to ask him about his opinion with regard to the girl. Left with no other option, Vijay had uninterestingly given his consent for the marriage. Slowly, he forgot the whole incident like it was a bad dream as he never got to see Parvathy or her daughter after that. He had started enjoying his life with Swathi and his daughter Ramya. But fate had suddenly given him a severe blow by snatching away his loved ones leaving him all alone in the world. He realized that God had indeed punished him for his brutal act. And now that he had come face to face with Priya, he wished to seek forgiveness from her...

Vijay picked up the photo lying on the table and started examining it once again. It was his own photo which was taken way back when he was twenty years old. He observed that Vikram looked exactly like him now and a lot of his features resembled his. He then began racking his brains. *Did Priya abort the baby or not? If for some reason, she had not done so, then probably Vikram was his son!* He was bow bent upon finding the truth; more than ever. He decided to visit Priya again.

# 33

The twilight of the day was slowly turning into darkness. Priya walked back into the kitchen after seeing Vikram off for his night shift. She gulped down the coffee which had turned cold; all the while feeling elated that Vikram had kept his word and had not gone to the hotel to meet Vijay. However, her happiness was short-lived.

Watching all the serials on the television and enjoying its vicarious pleasures had become a favourite pastime for Priya. She was just about to switch on the television when all of a sudden she saw Vijay standing at her door step.

"Can I come in?" He asked flashing a smile at her. Priya froze in panic and her entire body stiffened. Gathering up courage she screamed, "Go away from here immediately!"

Unperturbed by her impoliteness, Vijay continued to wait outside the house for her to calm down and give her consent, not willing to barge in. Seeing that Vijay was in no way going to budge from there, she folded her palms together and begged, "Please leave me alone! I do not want anything to do with you!"

Vijay was quick to realise that Priya was in fact too intimidated by his presence. Taking the liberty, he started walking slowly towards her, not heeding to her please; for he was determined to know the truth from her, what so ever. Priya's eyes at once widened with immense anger and she went berserk, stamping around the house in great fury. "How dare you enter my house? Haven't I told you that I despise you a lot, so much so that I don't even wish to see your face?" She exclaimed violently.

Impassive towards her fleeting temper, Vijay stood there; silently observing her frenzies. When her attempts to send him out failed, Priya decided to take the lead. She started heading towards the door when suddenly, she felt Vijay's strong hands on her. He caught her wrist and pulled her back. Despite her squirming, he did not loosen his grip and said in a low voice, "Priya, don't overreact! Please understand! I am at present in a state of depression as fate has given a severe blow to me by taking away my loved ones, leaving me forlorn and desperate. I am not the rough and arrogant person I used to be and as you remember. I have become a subdued man and I am not here to give you any trouble. So, please stop hurting me with your sharp words. If at all I had behaved in a ruthless manner with you, it was because of infatuation. You had a strange effect on me and I had lost all my sense of values when it came to you. While God has given us the brain to experience the various sorts of feelings, he has not given us the power switch to control our emotions and makes it run haywire. That exactly is the cause for all our problems."

Priya softened a little but however was much disgusted by the fact that he was still holding her hand. Trying to pull away from him, she asked curtly, "What is it that you want from me now? By any chance, if you have come to see Vikram, he is not here and has already left for work."

Releasing her hand at last, he said in a humble voice, "Priya, please don't be so rude to me. Actually, I am here to see you. I know that Vikram would have gone for work. That's why I have come to meet you because it is regarding Vikram that I wish to talk to you."

*The dreadful moment has at last arrived. Once he learns that Vikram is his son, surely he is going to impinge his rights on him and snatch him away from her. Well, it was she who had made the terrible mistake of coming back to Chennai for the sake of Vikram. There was no point in repenting now.*

Suddenly her face turned serious and she said quietly, "What is it you want to know about him?"

"Well......actually I am stricken with grief and am lamenting at the loss of my family, when I had the chance to meet Vikram. I was really fascinated by him so much that I looked forward to having a small chat with him every day. On his birthday, when I appreciated the golden watch he was wearing, he proudly showed it to me saying that his mother treasured it as a priceless gift as it was given to her by his father who is no more. I had noticed the name Venketeswaran on it and since then I have lost my sleep. I wish to know ........"

The moment he referred to the golden watch, Priya's whole body trembled. Tears blurred her vision and words failed her. She understood what was running in his mind and what he intended to know. Trying to get a hold on herself, she said softly, "Yes, Vikram is your son!" Further reserving all her fears and doubts to herself, she revealed everything to him. "Your father disposed of my mother that day with the golden watch asking her to mortgage or sell it and use the money for aborting the child clandestinely. My mother returned home heart broken and she was glum the whole night and did not talk much to me. The next morning, she did not wake up. She had suffered a massive heart attack in the middle of night. Then, it was my neighbour's daughter Radha who had been of great help to me. Not having the heart to forsake me all alone, she requested me to accompany her to Mumbai. While she was away at work, I helped her with the household chores and also took care of her son. It was she who had counseled me and advised me not to abort the child. Being all alone, bereft of any kith and kin, I obliged to her advice, so that I could have someone to call of my own and hence decided to give birth to Vikram. And as Vikram was growing up, I did not wish to be a burden to her and opted to move out on my own. Once again, it was Radha who got me a job in the Arts College where she was working......"

Priya paused a moment for her voice started to quiver all of a sudden. She felt so disgraced to tell him about the life she had been leading all these years. However, she did not wish to hide anything from him. *Her image was sure to get tarnished in his eyes. Probably this would create an aversion in his mind and distance him from her. She could then be free from his clutches for the rest of her life!* Slowly and hesitantly, she confessed, "I had to stoop very low for work and did a job of posing as a nude model in order to bring up Vikram in a comfortable manner." She broke down and was weeping vociferously.

*It was a delightful moment for Vijay. He felt ecstatic to hear that Vikram was his own son. He had been undergoing a long spell of dullness in life. He had reached that moment in his life when he had lost hope and thought that there was going to be no sunshine in his life ever. For the first time he felt the urge to live in this world. He felt alive.*

Vijay was once again in love with her all of a sudden. He longed to stay by her side and help her lead a happy and peaceful life. That's the only way; he could seek salvation in this life! Patting her on the shoulder, he pacified her, "Priya, please stop crying now. I am extremely sorry for all the mental agony you had to undergo because of me." Priya immediately wiped away her tears and tried to compose herself when he further continued, "I am really amazed to note that unlike me, all these difficulties and challenging times have made you a strong person. You have indeed emerged as a fine human being." Priya made an effort to smile and continued standing there in silence; basking in his accolade when suddenly Vijay moved closer to her. Holding her chin in his hands, he said staring right into her eyes, "Priya, I still love you for what you are! Consider all your problems and worries blown away by the winds. Of course, we can never go back and repair the past which is impossible, but we can construct a new future for us...."

Priya was stunned by what he was getting at and she immediately pulled away from him. "That would never be possible at all! We are from very different backgrounds and ...."

Vijay interrupted her hastily, "Why isn't it possible? Don't you know that true love does not know any class, creed or culture! Can't you see that we belong to each other? Probably it is God's wish that we should be together. Everything has been a perfect coincidence. Could fate have concocted a more bizarre way for us to meet?" "That you should come and work for me ....That the missing watch should result in the birth of Vikram........ That after twenty long years, Vikram should walk into my hotel and I should take an instant fascination for him ........and that my eyes should fall on his golden watch resulting in our reunion. Surely, our coming together is something very holy and divine!"

Priya's face turned pale and she broke into a sweat all of a sudden. Vijay was quick to notice the resentment on her face and hence continued, "Well, I do not wish to force you into taking a quick decision. You may take your time and think about it." He paused to add before leaving, "My doors are always open for you and you can walk in any time you wish. I shall be there to receive you with open arms!"

# 34

For some unknown reason, Priya was fllled with a pang of remorse when she saw Vijay leave. She noted that the tragedy of his life had transformed him tremendously and he had indeed become a very humble person. In fact, she was able to speak bravely in front of him and was not afraid of him anymore. She realised that he would cause no trouble to her. Suddenly, she experienced a shiver of excitement at his proposition. Her face brightened up with a smile. She was unable to wipe the smile off her face for the rest of the day.

Early next morning, Priya was eagerly waiting for Vikram to come home as she wanted to apprise him about Vijay's visit. But then she changed her mind instantly on seeing the worried expression on his face. Without having his usual tete-a-tete with her, Vikram straightaway went to have his bath. When Vikram continued to be quite even while having his breakfast, Priya asked, "Is anything wrong? You look so tensed."

"Yes Ma! I have bad news for you and please don't get shattered with what I am going to say." He said as Priya stared at him restlessly. "Due to the ongoing recession, my company is laying-off a few people and my name appears in the list as I am a new comer."

It was indeed devastating news for her. However concealing the shock, she said rather coolly, trying to comfort him, "So what? You can try elsewhere and you are sure to get a better job than this. Don't take this rejection to your heart." Vikram felt glad that his mother was unruffied by the news and further continued, "You are indeed right. My other two friends have already found a new job and they are asking me also to join them. But I refused since the job is at Bangalore and moreover they are demanding a security deposit of Rupees one lakh which we certainly cannot afford."

Not willing to see her son in a depressed mood, Priya said without any hesitation, "If you wish, you may also go along with them." Vikram was thrilled to hear his mother say that. "Are you sure I can go to Bangalore?" He asked thinking that his mother must be joking. When he saw her nod, Vikram sprang out of his chair and affectionately gave her a warm hug. Priya shoved him away to warn him kindly, "But you must promise to visit me every weekend. And once you are settled, I shall also accompany you."

"I shall deflnitely come here every weekend." Vikram said grinning happily. However he became morose once again and asked with much concern in his voice, "But where do we go for the money to pay the security deposit?"

"Don't keep grumbling all the time. That shall be taken care of." Priya said frowning at him. After a short while, she returned with the golden watch. Handing it over to him she said, "You may pledge this in a reliable pawn broker's shop and get the required money and redeem it later when we are flnancially sound." Vikram was on cloud nine and he said, "Ma, I did not even imagine that you will take this whole issue so sportively. I thank you with all my heart for your magnanimity. I have the best mother in this world!"

# 35

Life had been posing one challenge one after another for Priya. In the beginning, whenever a new challenge sprang up in her life, she had been overwhelmed by it. But now slowly, she had learnt to rise from every setback and put herself in sync with the moment.

When Vikram informed her that he had lost his job, Priya was in fact shaken up by the news but she did not express her shock to him. However, she couldn't bear to see him in low spirits and for this she was prepared to do anything. That's why she had let him go far away to Bangalore and that too after pledging her golden watch which was so dear to her.

Priya had deliberated at length on the subject of Vijay's proposal; weighing all the pros and cons she finally arrived at a conclusion that it was really not feasible. Firstly, Priya never believed in luck. She always considered herself unlucky. She was at present leading a satisfactory life. By stepping into his house of grandeur and riches, her life style was sure to undergo a drastic change. Her now contented life would be thrown out of gear all of a sudden. Hence she kept silent over this and did not discuss anything about Vijay's visit or about his proposal to Vikram.

Vikram was true to his word and visited her every weekend and also spoke to her every night before going to bed, recounting the entire day's happenings. Hence Priya did not feel his absence. However, it was during the second month that problems cropped up resulting in a misunderstanding between the mother and son so much so that Priya regretted sending Vikram to Bangalore.

For he stopped visiting her during the weekends and his phone calls also became sporadic. Whenever Priya tried to contact him, he either did not take the call or told her that he would call her later and never bothered to call back. When Priya once shouted at him for his uncaring attitude, he informed her that he was swarmed with a lot of work and was too busy. Frustrated over this, Priya stopped calling him.

Suddenly doubts began to assail her mind. *Was he seeing any girl? Was he distracted by her? Surely boys considered their girlfriends to be more superior to their mothers!* Priya became upset over this. Though Priya was much disturbed by Vikram's lackadaisical attitude, she did not wish to share her anxiety or fears with anyone.

# 36

One Saturday evening, Priya was sitting outside her house, cupping her chin in her hands. She had been waiting and was on pins and needles since morning for Vikram's arrival. It had been almost a month now and Priya was dying to see him. Vikram had promised to be there in the morning but had still not turned up. The delay was making her tense. How could he be so irresponsible not to keep her informed of the changes?

*Loving people and forming close bonds only result in great pain when they are separated from us.* Vikram was the cause of her present mental tension. Of late, he seemed to be avoiding her by not answering her calls and also by not visiting her during weekends on the pretext of work.

*Expectations! It is one of the most dreadful feelings that God bestows on human beings!* Did she not know that expectations brought ony failures with them? When her dreams of going to college and later for a job in order to take care of her mother were shattered, Priya had become despondent. She felt so desperate then as though she were sailing in a ship that was about to sink. Luckily, she did not perish, for Radha had turned out to be her life savior and had helped her cross the turbulent sea of life smoothly. Priya had blindly followed the advice given by Radha entrusting her life into her hands and that's how she had landed up in Mumbai, given birth to Vikram and had taken up the job of being nude model. She had learned to live life one day at a time; adapting herself to any situation.

She kept pondering whether she was expecting too much from Vikram? Vikram was now a grown up man and perhaps he wants to be left alone. It was only unfair on her part to expect him to be with her all the time. *May be it was time to let him go!*

Priya took out the letter from the envelope and started reading it for the umpteenth time. It was her appointment letter for the position of an Assistant at *Meenakshi Old age Home.* Priya had approached them a few weeks back and had volunteered to offer her services in any possible manner. Maya the owner of the old age home had promised to get back to her.

The words said by Maya at once came to her mind. Maya, who was in her late flfties; was a pious and religious lady. Widowed at a young age and with her son settled in the States, she had come up with the idea of setting up an old age home instead of wallowing in self-pity. She had informed Priya that this gave her a sense of satisfaction. Appreciating Priya's enthusiasm, she had said, "The earthly residence is not our real home. It was not ours before and after sometime; it will again not be ours. One day, we all have to depart from here, leaving everything behind. Our real home is where we will live forever – that is in the heart of God. And one way to achieve this is to offer your services to His children; however small it might be, without expectations and in a detached manner. After all, service to mankind is the rent you pay to God for your life on earth. This will remove your entire ego and lead you to liberation. You are sure to reach God no doubt and stay in his permanent abode." Priya had been enamored by her words and had returned home happy. She had never thought that she would get such a quick response from Maya.

The evening was slowly turning into twilight and the prayers of the *Muezzin* from the nearby Mosque fiooded across and drifted into the still night. Priya folded the letter and put it back into the envelope. She was determined to take up this job. That way she will not be bothering her son too much. Apart from that, she could also lead an independent life without being a burden to him.

Just as she stood up, she saw a car stop in front of her house.

# 37

When she saw Vijay getting down from the car, she was astounded. *Why was he here now? Perhaps he wished to find out her decision regarding his proposal?* He was striding fast towards her and Priya invited him with a smile. But Vijay did not return her smile as he was cut up with her. He was aware that Priya was neglecting him, for she had neither bothered to call him up nor send Vikram to meet him. He followed her silently.

Once they were alone inside the house, Vijay asked, "What the hell is wrong with you? You didn't care to call me even once during these two months." While Priya was wondering what reply to give him, he immediately went close to her and placing his hands over her shoulders asked, "Now tell me, is there any chance of luck regarding my proposal to you? Have you made up your mind to come and stay with me?"

Priya was taken aback by his sudden gesture. Vijay was standing too close to her and she was unable to think coherently. Her heart started pounding and she became speechless. Not having received an answer, he pulled her closer to him and continued in a low voice, "Priya, please don't be silent. Feel free to open your heart to me." At once her face flushed with excitement over his intimacy and she stammered, "Well... I need some more time to....."

Interrupting her, he asked exerting his authority, "Are you going to take your whole life time to decide about it?"

Noticing that Vijay was not going to leave her until she gave him a convincing reply, she mumbled, "Actually.... Vikram is not around here. He has gone to Bangalore for a job and I did not have the opportunity of discussing this subject with him. Once he comes....."

"And when will that be?" He snapped at her not letting her finish.

Priya was quiet for a while before she continued, "I am not sure about that. Vikram is nowadays too busy with his job and has no time for me. The moment I get to see him, I shall talk to him about this and get back to you."

"And what if that moment happens to be now? Will you promise to give me some good news right away?" He asked smiling at her.

"Of ourse!" Priya nodded staring at him uncomprehendingly.

Vijay immediately summoned his driver who came running to him. He whispered something to him and the driver swiftly walked towards the car and opened the door. Priya was in for a great surprise! Immediately, Vikram came out of the car, grinning with his smile stretching from one ear to the other.........

# 38

The pawn broker *sait* Lalchand was rummaging the large jewel box. He had returned after a long religious tour and had just taken over from his son. He wished to know if there were any additions to the jewel box that were pledged by people during his absence. That is when the golden watch studded with diamonds caught his eyes. Since the watch looked so familiar to him he took it out and observed it closely. When he saw the name Venketeswaran on it, he was stumped. At once, his memory sprang back to the past.

Venketeswaran had many a times pledged this golden watch with him during the financial constraints he faced while running his hotel business. However, it was a well-known fact that once his son Vijay had taken over from him, he had modernised the hotel so well and it was now flourishing well. That being the case, Lalchand was perplexed as to how this watch landed up here. He contacted his son immediately who informed him that a young lad by named Vikram had pledged this watch seeking a loan of rupees one lakh to pay for his security deposit for a job at Bangalore. Lalchand was once again plunged in doubts. He was aware that Vijay had lost his family in the Tsunami and was leading a single life. Being a family friend, he had also gone to meet Vijay and offered his condolences to him. Now, he wondered in what way this boy Vikram connected with *The Venketeswara Quality Inn*. His curiosity got the better of him...

Vijay had been thinking of Vikram day in and day out. It had been nearly a month since Vikram had visited him and he was much perturbed about this. He was now yearning to see him and kept pondering over as to why Vikram was avoiding him;, it was then that his phone rang. It was from his father's old friend *Sait* Lalchand. On hearing the entire story from him, Vijay rushed to meet him in person. He divulged all the facts relating to his past and also confessed to him that Vikram was his own son. Further, he redeemed the watch after paying rupees one lakh and obtained the address where Vikram was presently staying at Bangalore.

Vijay was amazed at the perfect circles life could draw. He had been longing to see his son and have an open-hearted discussion with him and here there was an opportunity, he thought. However, he first decided to give him a good piece of his mind for going away to Bangalore without putting a word to him and also for keeping him in the dark about his financial needs. Later, he wished to brief him about the proposal he had made to his mother and convince him that since his mother had in fact had many a heart wrenching experiences on account of him, he now wanted to make up for everything by keeping her eternally happy.

Vijay however, was in for a shock when he reached Bangalore. One of Vikram's roommates informed him that Vikram had met with an accident and was admitted in the hospital. He also explained to him that Vikram was rushing to work one morning when he had a head on collision with a speeding car and was thrown off his bike. Luckily, there was no danger to his life but his right leg was badly injured and required urgent surgery. The doctor had advised him to stay for two weeks in the hospital. He then accompanied Vijay to the hospital. On seeing Vijay, Vikram was shocked and his eyes were fllled up with tears. Vijay assured him that he would get well soon and also promised to stay with him in the hospital till his recovery.

During this short span of time, the father and son got to know each other very well. In fact, Vijay had a heart to heart talk with his son and apprised him about the proposal he had made to his mother. Further, he told him to resign his job and help him with the hotel business. Once Vikram was back on his feet, Vijay arranged to bring him back to Chennai by fiight....

# 39

There was a small bandage in his right leg and Vikram limped his way towards his mother. He was not sure if he would face hostility, amusement or evasion and so stood there silently for a while before he said quietly, "Ma, I met with a terrible accident and had to be admitted in the hospital for a foot surgery. I am sorry I kept lying to you all these days that I was busy with work. Actually, I did not want you to know about this because you would have been worried sick of me ...."

Upset that Vikram had kept her in the dark about his accident, she raised her voice, "This is not something you should hide from your mother. Had you informed me, I would have come over there and assisted you."

"But there was no necessity for that as my father was already taking good care of me." Vikram said beaming with a smile.

Priya gaped at Vijay disbelievingly when he stepped forward and fllled her in with the story. Priya was all ears for him and when he flnished narrating the facts to her, Vikram added rather enthusiastically, "Father has forced me to tender my resignation. He is just starting a fast food unit adjoining *The Venketeswara Quality Inn* and wants me to take care of it. He has also requested both of us to move in with him. We can all be together and there is no need for us to stay apart hereafter."

Priya did not respond to him but silently walked into the kitchen to prepare coffee for them. She kept thinking of Vikram all the while smiling to herself. He had very easily accepted Vijay as his father and acted as if they have been living together all their life and had never been apart. Surely, Vijay should have been molly cuddling him a lot for him to earn this love and respect from Vikram.

Priya was caught unaware when Vijay walked into the kitchen suddenly. Standing beside her, he asked, "Have I made you happy now? Your son is back and is going to stay with you. You are now left with no choice but to shift to my residence immediately; at least for the sake of Vikram, if not for me."

When Priya continued to be grim, he said rather curtly, "I have been promising you time and again that my only endeavor in this life now is to keep you and Vikram happy but you really don't seem to appreciate my feelings at all."

"Actually, I have other plans in life..." Priya drawled.

"What plans do you have in mind?" Vijay asked when suddenly his eyes fell on the envelope lying beside the gas stove. Even without seeking her permission, he pulled out the letter and started reading it. The letter from Meenakshi Old age Home was addressed to her :

*"This is with reference to your interview that you had with us in connection with offering your services to our old age home. We are pleased to inform you that you have been selected for the job of an Assistant. We look forward to your association with us."*

Handing it back to her, he asked, "Is this your problem? You want to be of service to people?"

"Not exactly, In fact, I wish to seek redemption from the sin I was forced to do."

Vijay blinked and staredat her for a while and then said, "What do you mean by that?"

Priya hesitated before she said, "Well, for sustenance of my life, I had to work as a nude model and was forced to bare my body in front of the art students. I might have indeed been useful to the young and budding artists who were having great ambitions in life. In fact they had frequently thanked me for the service I was doing for them. However, deep inside my heart there is an embedded feeling of guilt. Fate had dealt a severe blow on me! At times, whenever I think about the life I was compelled to lead, I feel ashamed of myself. Now, I would like to even the score by being of service to the old people who have to leave their families and loved ones for some reason or the other and stay alone in the old age home. All that these people yearn for is love. I would like to end my life by caring for these old people who are waiting for their call from God."

"End your life?" Vijay sneered at her.

"You are just thirty eight years and you are talking about ending your life now itself! In fact, it is me who should seek redemption from the sins I have done in my life! Well, I do understand your feelings but there is still time for it, Priya. Listen, there are moments when difficulties occur in our lives and we cannot avoid them. However, they occur for a reason. Only when we overcome them, do we understand why they happened in the first place. Our lives are the best example of that!"

Priya was stunned at his philosophical explanation as he further continued, "Well I am now drawing out plans for both of us to live together and start life afresh and so please try and come out of the past. First of all, I wish to take you to the Registration office on an auspicious day and register our marriage so that you can legally become my wife."

Priya was startled by his plans. He was not even consulting her or seeking her opinion and taking decisions on his own. She realised that he was in no way going to let her pursue her career of working as an Assistant in the Old age home. Not giving her an opportunity to voice her views on his plans, he continued, "As Vikram told you earlier, I am opening a new fast food unit adjoining the hotel and he is going to be in charge of it. You can give him ideas of healthy and traditional recipes. This way, you will still be doing service to people and enter their hearts through their stomach!"

Priya smiled in response. Embracing her from behind, he said, "Who knows what is in store for us in the future. It is only the present which is in our hands. Let us start to enjoy life by learning to live for the moment. And if our son ever ditches us in our old age, then we shall together go and join The Meenakshi Old age Home."

Priya was too embarrassed by his proximity and she tried to pull away from him for fear that Vikram would bump into them. Vijay was offended by this and he turned her around forcefully to face her and said, "Why do you look so pale? Do you still have any reservations regarding the decision to lead your life with me? I see no joy in your face. Now, tell me one thing honestly, Priya. Are you not happy in joining me?"

"Not really....." She said rather shyly.

"Thanks Priya. That's enough for me. I don't wish to hear anything further from you."

Then drawing her closer to him once again, he scolded, "In that case, will you please stop fussing over like this whenever I get close to you." Priya remained silent and stood there blushing. Perhaps Vijay was able to drive home his point this time, for she did not resist further as he held her close in his arms. In fact, she felt a new strength flow into her all of a sudden. Was this strange feeling she was experiencing called love, she wondered. After placing a light kiss on her forehead, he withdrew abruptly. Vijay was in fact much elated. He felt as though a cool and fresh breeze had blown into his rather stale life all of a sudden.

He swiftly left the room to join Vikram to discuss his future plans with him.

# 40

Priya was brimming with excitement about the new developments in her life. For a moment, she wondered how this new life was going to be. Her mind was suddenly filled with doubts. *What if he continued to torment her and make her life miserable?* But immediately, she reassured herself thinking that she was capable of tackling any problem in life now? The most difficult times have made her who she was today. She has emerged as a stronger person.

She suddenly got a hold on herself. She decided to accept this situation gracefully. She told herself, “Hey, Life, let’s see you get on me this time! After all, was this not what her mother had taught her – both during her life time and through her death? To face challenges in a courageous manner!

In a short while, Priya came in carrying a tray with coffee for both of them. While helping himself with a cup of coffee, Vikram, proudly showed off the golden watch he was wearing and said, “Ma, look at this! Doesn’t it look fabulous on my hand?” He paused before saying, “And Ma, you are not getting it back. This exclusively belongs to me. After all, you have my father with you now; take care of him nicely. Treasure him for the rest of your life; for he is your priceless gift!” Vikram’s words rejuvenated Priya’s spirits and removed all her inhibitions and fears. She felt so light and suddenly free!

*******************